Mine to Protect

Pine Ridge Pack:
Book 3

Jayda Marx

D1307936

Author's Note

Thank you for your interest in my book! This paranormal romance features my take on some seriously sexy wolf shifters. They share many attributes of shifters found in other fictional works, but not all. This is the third and final installment of the "Pine Ridge Pack" series, and they are best read in order. This book contains fated mates, sweet moments and lots of laughs. My stories are low angst and **insta-love.** They follow **relationships on the fast track**, and I live for sweetness! I want my readers to finish my books with a smile on their face and a fierce case of the warm and fuzzies. Laughter is guaranteed, and each read delivers its own type of drama. Thanks again for taking a look and happy reading!

Chapter One

Wren

I smiled when I pulled into Preston's driveway and saw that his car was still there. My boyfriend worked during evening hours as a police officer while I worked dayshift, so it could be difficult to find a good time to get together. But today, my boss let me leave a few minutes early and I wanted to surprise Preston with the treat I brought for him; a big slab of peanut butter pie from the diner where I worked. It was his favorite.

The diner was where Preston and I met nearly a month ago. I was covering a late shift for my co-worker because her baby was sick, and Preston came in with his partner on their lunch break. He chatted and even flirted with me while they ate and I was floored when he asked me out.

Even though I was an adult, having turned twenty a few months ago, I had very little experience with men. And by very little I mean zero. I came from a home where being gay was *not* acceptable, so I wasn't able to explore the dating scene until I branched out on my own.

Even though my parents forbade me to date men, I suppose I could have experimented with secret hookups, but that sort of thing never interested me. I was curious but not desperate. Of course I wanted sex; I was a twenty year old man. But sex wasn't all I wanted. I wanted a relationship with a special someone. And that's why I was so excited when Preston took me to dinner for my first ever date.

Because of our schedules, we'd only been out a couple of times. Even though things were new, I liked Preston. He was nice and very handsome, with black hair and dark brown eyes. He was taller than me (most people were, considering I was only five foot four inches) and strong. I liked the idea of being with a strong guy; it made me feel safe, especially since I was so small. Not only was I short, but I only weighed a whopping one hundred twenty pounds. I could barely fight off a mosquito, so I liked feeling protected.

The only problem Preston and I faced so far was that he was older than I was and more experienced. It was no secret that he wanted sex; he brought it up often and didn't understand why I turned him down when he asked. But I told him repeatedly that I wasn't ready, and he didn't force me. We'd kissed and cuddled, but nothing more.

I climbed out of my car and hurried to his doorstep with his pie in my hands. I wanted to sit with him while he ate his snack and talk to him for a bit before he left for work. I knocked on his front door but there was no answer. *Uh oh, I hope he didn't oversleep.* He liked to stay up and play games on his computer after his shift and then sleep in. I knocked harder, but again there was no answer.

I didn't want him to get in trouble at his job; I needed to wake him up, so I tried his doorknob. It was unlocked, and the door squeaked as it opened. I didn't want to barge in or startle him, so I pulled my phone from my pocket and dialed his number. It rang several times before going to voicemail. I called him again, and this time he picked up on the fourth ring.

"*What?*" he snapped, making me flinch.

"H-hey, Preston," I stuttered, shocked at the greeting. "I'm sorry; did I wake you up?"

"Oh, Wren, I'm sorry baby. I didn't mean to snap at you." I smiled at the nickname and instantly forgave him. "I'm just having a rough day at work."

I blinked over at his car in confusion. "You're at work?" He always drove himself because his co-workers lived in the opposite direction, so carpooling wouldn't make sense.

"I just said I was," he replied in a snippy tone.

"Oh...okay. Well, I-" before I could explain that I was there to visit, I heard a man's voice in the background. Only he wasn't speaking; he was grunting and groaning. My face went numb and icy coldness gripped my chest. Preston *was* at home, but he wasn't alone. *He's cheating on me.* Apparently he couldn't wait until I was ready and found some ass on the side.

"Look, I'll call you later," Preston said and ended the call before I could say another word.

Tears ran down my cheeks and I gripped my phone in a shaking hand. The first guy I liked turned out to be a spectacular douche, and my first relationship went straight to hell.

My heart dropped at the sight of the pie in my hand. I'd tried to do something sweet for him only to discover this. Anger bubbled inside my gut and I shoved my phone in my pocket before angrily wiping my face. This wasn't time to cry; it was time to get even. The door was already open; I'd march right into his bedroom and smash the pie in his cheating face.

I gave a determined nod and stomped across the threshold and down the hall. I knew where his bedroom was; he tried to get me to go in there with him one day when I was over watching movies. He just rolled his eyes when I said no. I was more glad than ever that I didn't sleep with him.

I burst into his bedroom just to find an empty, neatly made bed. *What? Where is he?* I searched every room, but there was no sign of him. *Maybe he really is at work; maybe he took a rideshare or something and I just caught him at a bad moment on the phone.*

I suddenly felt very guilty for wanting to smash the pie in his face. *I'll put this in his fridge and we'll laugh about my wild imagination later.*

But as I walked into his kitchen, I heard a long, loud moan coming from beneath me. *He is here! And he's turned his basement into a sex dungeon!* My fury returned and I yanked the basement door open.

I marched down the stairs, but I didn't see anything out of the ordinary. There was no sex dungeon; just boxes, a washer and dryer and normal basement stuff. There was, however, a door on the opposite side of the room which was cracked open. The grunting sound was coming from within the small enclosed room behind the door.

I crept across the floor, trying to be quiet so I could catch Preston in the act. But when I made it to the room and peeked through the cracked door, I wasn't prepared for what I saw.

Preston and his police partner Ricky loomed over a man on his knees. The man's face was so bruised and swollen that I couldn't recognize him even if I knew him. All I could tell was that he wore a police uniform.

"I hate doing this, Mick," Preston said before kicking the guy in the stomach. The familiar grunting sound sprung from his bloodied lips. "We had a good thing going. We all got an equal cut; you, me, Ricky,

Stan, Gene, and Andrew. But what happened?"

"You got greedy," Ricky cut in. "And told Stan you'd squeal if you didn't get a bigger cut. Bad move, Mick." He backhanded the guy and my stomach turned. I'd never seen violence like this in real life.

Just from the quick conversation, I gathered they were dirty cops taking bribes or drug money or...something. I didn't know specifics and I didn't want them. All I knew was that things were over between me and Preston, and that I wanted to help Mick. He should go to jail for whatever he did, not be treated like this. I put my hand on the door to push it open and stop Preston and Ricky; to shield Mick while I called an ambulance, but I froze when Preston pulled a gun from his waistband.

"You can't be trusted, Mick." A loud pop shook the walls when Preston fired his weapon, and Mick's limp body collapsed onto the floor.

The dessert I was still dumbly holding fell from my hands and splattered on the cement floor. *Oh god, he's dead. I just saw someone die.* Large, hot tears rolled down my face. I couldn't move; my body was frozen in shock.

"What do we do with the body?" Ricky asked.

"We'll dump it downtown and it'll be chalked up to gang violence. He'll get a medal of honor for going in the line of service. It's better than the greedy bastard deserves."

I slowly walked backwards, wanting to run out of the room but unable to make my feet understand. I gasped when I bumped into a box and knocked it over, sending tools clanging loudly over the floor. *Fuck!*

"What was that?" Ricky's voice asked.

"Let's check it out," Preston replied as he cocked his gun again. *Fuck, fuck, fuck.*

I didn't have time to run; I wouldn't even get out of the room before they caught me, so I dodged behind a stack of boxes. Luckily my small body was easily hidden.

I watched through cracks between the boxes as Preston and Ricky came out into the main area of the basement. Preston's shirt was speckled with blood. He crouched down and inspected the smeared pie on the cement.

"Wren was here."

"Shit. Do you think he saw?"

"Of course he fucking saw. Otherwise he'd still be here. He's probably still in the house. We have to find him."

"And when we do?"

"We can't have him blab. Kill him." I covered my mouth with both hands to hold back the sound of my sobs.

"Dude, that's cold," Ricky replied. "Knocking off your own boyfriend?"

"Eh, I popped his sweet little cherry; that's all I wanted anyway." I nearly jumped out and called him a damn liar, but it would only get me a bullet in the head like poor Mick, so I stayed hidden. "It's too bad; he was fun to play with."

"Then maybe we can *both* play with him before we take him out," Ricky suggested as he grabbed his gun as well.

Preston laughed and nodded his head. "Come on, let's go get him." I couldn't believe the monster I'd gotten involved with, or the company he kept. How could they kill a man over something as trivial as money? And how could Preston - someone who was *supposed* to care about me - value my life so little?

The moment they disappeared up the stairs, I swiftly and silently came out from behind the boxes and searched the room for a way out. *Yes!* Just under the ceiling on the far wall was a small window which I may be able to fit through.

I dragged a plastic storage container to the wall and climbed on top. I stretched my arms over my head, but couldn't quite reach the window. My heart beat wildly in my chest when I heard the heavy footsteps above me as Preston and Ricky searched the house.

I stacked another plastic tub onto the first one and clambered to the top. They rocked beneath my feet, but I managed to keep my balance. I was also able to reach the window. I flipped the lock and pushed on the glass, but it was stuck. It had probably never been opened.

"His car's still here," Preston's voice called from upstairs. "He *has* to be here somewhere."

"We've searched every room," Ricky argued.

There was a moment of silence before Preston concluded, "The little shit is in the basement."

Come on, come on, I silently begged the window as I shoved the glass with all of my might. Finally, the frame creaked and the window swung outward. I had zero muscle tone, but the adrenaline rush of the moment gave me enough strength to pull my body up the wall. I wriggled my small body through the opening; it was a tight fit, but I squeezed out onto the grass.

As I rose to my feet, I heard the pair stampeding down the stairs inside, and Preston yell, "He went out the window!"

I ran as fast as I could towards the treeline in the distance; the area where we lived had a lot of forests, so at least I'd have places to hide.

I may have been able to get to my car before the duo made it out of the house, but they'd hunt me down. They could put out an alert on my vehicle and have every police officer looking for me. I was confident that there were good cops out there too, but I didn't know who I could trust or how large Preston's circle of corruption was.

He'd told me all about the ways he was able to track down criminals; not only by tagging their vehicles, but by tracing phones and watching for banking activity. I pulled my cell phone from my pocket and threw it on the ground so that they'd have no way to track me. I didn't throw my wallet; I just wouldn't use my credit cards. What sucked was the fact that I never carried cash. I used my debit card for everything. But now I couldn't even withdraw money or get something to eat because Preston could find me. Not that I had plans to go back into the city. For now, my only plan was to stay in tree cover.

My breath puffed out in front of me as I ran into the woods at top speed. It was freezing outside. The wind cut my cheeks and burned my lungs, but I couldn't stop. I had to put as much distance between myself and Preston as possible. I had no plan or destination; *I just have to keep running*.

Chapter Two

Stone

I drained the last of my beer and placed the empty bottle back on the bar. I was enjoying a little peace and quiet before I began my shift on the trails; it was hard to come by lately. I was just thrilled that the Christmas season was over; I'd never heard such a ruckus in all of my life.

Rory and Dax *loved* the holiday, and from the day after Halloween, they forced me to watch every goddamn Christmas movie in existence with them, bake cookies and decorate trees. When I told them I didn't want a tree in *my* home, they just laughed and bought me the biggest one the store had to offer, claiming I needed "extra cheer".

The worst part was when they decided they wanted to go caroling. Rowan and Phoenix joined them because they're dick whipped and do anything their mates want, while nearly breaking their neck in the process to make sure they do it quickly enough. Well, since all four of them decided to sing and there's only five of us living in the state park, guess who their audience was? I stood there in the cold for a fucking hour listening to them sing "Jingle Bells" and a song about a reindeer with a glowing face. It was ridiculous. Eventually, I locked my door and went to bed with pillows crammed over my ears.

It's not that I hate Christmas. And it's certainly not that I hate Dax or Rory; just the opposite. They, along with Phoenix and Rowan, are my pack; my brothers. I love them all. I love getting together several times a week for our pack dinners and just shooting the shit. I'd never tell them this, but I even liked baking cookies. Caroling was a step too far.

The main problem was that even though I was happy that Rowan and Phoenix found their mates, it was hard watching the four of them go all giggles and googly-eyes over each other all the damn time. And if I were honest with myself, it was difficult because I wanted that too; the mate, not the giggles.

All shifters want their mate; they're a gift from Fate of a partner to share our immortal lives with. They complete our broken souls, soothe our hearts, and give us a purpose in our lives; to provide for, love and protect them.

For the longest time, I was in no hurry to meet my mate. I had fun playing the field and sowing my wild oats. But watching the four of my packmates together, I realized that meaningless sex with countless strangers was just that; meaningless. Seeing the smiles on my friends' faces and knowing the contentment in their hearts, it was impossible not to want that for myself. I didn't regret my wild past, but I was ready for something deeper. Now came the hardest part; being patient and waiting for Fate to deliver. I was positive her delivery wasn't the twink currently eye fucking me from across the bar.

"Hey big boy," he greeted as he sashayed up to the stool beside me. "If you ask nicely, I'll let you buy me a drink."

How generous of you. "I just ran out of money," I lied, and he pushed his bottom lip into a pout. There was nothing wrong with the guy. Actually, he was just my type; small, blond and cute. I'm a prideful bastard and enjoy towering over my men. It makes me feel large and in charge. I hoped my mate was small and needed me to protect him from the world. Thinking of my potential mate made the thought of hooking up with this guy turn my stomach, which was new for me.

"But that guy looks loaded," I told him while nodding to a man at the end of the bar who was wearing an expensive dress shirt. He was also giving the small man a very obvious once over. "And thirsty."

"Hmm, that he does," he replied before flitting over to the other man. By the time I got my tab settled, the two of them were sucking face. *That didn't take long.* I rolled my eyes as I zipped my coat, and stepped out into the frigid evening.

*****

I parked the pack's SUV near our cabins and noticed that only Dax and Rowan's home was illuminated from the inside. That probably meant that Phoenix and Rory were visiting, and that I should keep my distance. The foursome were already gearing up for Valentine's Day with movies, candy and decorations, and I didn't want any part of that mushfest.

As long as there were no large branches fallen over the paths, my trail visit should be quick; nobody was dumb enough to be straggling behind in this weather. The temperature could easily drop to single digits in mid-January, and that was *without* the wind chill.

I could check the paths quicker in wolf form, but my gut told me to stay in human form; maybe there was a fallen branch that needed removed or something. So, as I walked past the treeline, I kept my eyes peeled for anything out of the ordinary.

I wasn't far into my search when a familiar scent hit my nostrils; smoke. I looked up to the sky and found a small black cloud billowing above the trees. I bolted towards the sight; the bark of the trees was dry and brittle this time of year and flames could spread quickly.

As I ran through the woods dodging low branches, I wondered how the hell a fire started in the first place. *It has to be man made.* My suspicions were confirmed when I burst into a clearing and found the small figure of a man huddled around a fire.

When the man saw me, he jumped to his feet and kicked snow on the flames, extinguishing them quickly before he ran towards a thick clump of trees.

I yelled, "Stop!", but the fucker just ran faster. He was quick, but too bad for him I had shifter speed. I caught up to him effortlessly and snatched him around the middle, lifting his feet from the ground.

I rolled my eyes as he kicked and screamed and flailed his arms. It was doing him no good; I was so much bigger than him, it was as if I were holding a pissed off kitten who didn't want a bath.

But as he struggled, I caught his scent on the breeze. I hadn't registered it at first because it was similar to the fire itself; warm, smokey and woodsy. But there was something else; there was an underlying sweetness to his scent. He smelled like a marshmallow roasted over cedar planks.

The aroma was both comforting and invigorating at once. It sent my pulse into overdrive and the hair on my arms stood up in recognition. A laugh rumbled in my chest when I realized this little troublemaker was my mate.

"Oh god," the man squeaked at the sound. He struggled harder and begged, "Let me go!"

"Settle down." I shook him a little in my arms to try to calm him. I wasn't an expert on comforting people, and his fearful whimper was proof of that. "I'll put you down if you promise you won't run away."

"I promise," he replied quickly.

I placed him on his feet and turned him to face me. My breath caught at my first glimpse; he was gorgeous. He had smooth pale skin, ocean blue eyes and a button nose. His shaggy light blond hair was parted to the side and fell onto his forehead, and his pouty lips called to mine. The top of his head barely reached my nipple line and his body was rail thin. He was everything I'd dreamed of and more.

"Now, why are-" my words cut off when my mate turned around and dashed towards the treeline again. *Oh, for fuck's sake.* I caught up to him in a few long strides and scooped him into my arms again. "You said you wouldn't run away."

"I'm sorry! Please don't kill me. I'll do anything, just don't kill me!" He kicked the shit out of my shins, and I smiled at the way he fought me even though it was useless. I was confused at what the hell he was talking about, though.

"I'm not going to kill you just because you built a fire."

My mate stopped thrashing. "A fire? You're here because of my fire?"

What is happening right now? "Yes. I was out checking the trails and saw the smoke."

"Checking the...wait, am I inside the state park? Are you a park ranger?"

"Yes." It was essentially true, and the easiest way to explain things.

"Oh, thank god." His body sagged in relief, and was only supported by my arm around his stomach. The rest of him hung limp like a wet cloth.

"I'm going to put you down again," I hedged. "Since you know you're not going to die, you don't have to run. And we both know I can catch you if you do, so just...stay still, okay?" He nodded and I set him on the ground facing me again, making sure he was steady before I released him.

"I'm sorry about the fire," he started, wringing his hands in front of him. "But it was safe. I made sure to build it in a clear area away from the trees." I was impressed by his survival skills and fire safety, but it still didn't answer why he was there in the first place. "I promise I won't make another one."

"You'll freeze to death out here without a fire." Actually, he looked close to freezing to death now; he was dressed only in a light sweater and jeans, and his body was shivering from head to toe.

He flinched and his eyes widened when I reached for the zipper of my coat. "Easy." I held up my free hand as I slowly unzipped my jacket before peeling it off of me. His eyes widened even more at the sight of my body in a slim-fitting t-shirt, and I didn't even try to hide my smile. "Here." I wrapped the warm fabric around his shoulders and smiled at the way it hung to his knees.

"Thank you." My mate slipped his arms into the holes and hugged the material closer to his body, and my chest warmed at providing him comfort.

"I want you to come with me to my cabin. You can get warmed up and I'll make you something to eat."

He nodded and took a step forward before stopping dead in his tracks. "This is a trap! You *are* going to kill me! You're taking me to him so that *he* can kill me!" He tried to zoom away again, but he didn't make it very far before I had him in my grip.

"Who are you talking about? Who wants to kill you?" My voice was rough and gravelly as I asked; the thought of someone trying to harm my mate made my blood boil.

"I've said too much. Just let me go and forget you saw me." Once again he pummeled my shins.

"Stop that." I jostled him in my arms until he sighed and went limp again. There was no way in hell I was letting him go *or* forgetting about him, but I stopped myself from saying that because it would probably just scare him more. Instead, I took a deep breath to collect my thoughts; something that was rare for me.

"I promise I'm not going to hurt you. I have no idea who or what you're talking about." I'd insist that he tell me whenever we got to my cabin, but I had to get him there first. "Stick your hand in the interior pocket of that coat." He didn't move, and instead just gave me a suspicious look. "Go on." He blew out a breath and tucked his hand into the jacket. His jaw dropped when he pulled a serrated knife out of the pocket. "I keep that on me for protection. Now it's yours; if at any point you feel like I'm betraying you, you have my permission to stab the shit out of me." He nodded and clutched the knife in his fist.

"Now, I'm going to take you to my cabin. There's no one there waiting for us, I live alone, and I'm a good cook. You can take a hot shower and I'll make you some dinner. Do you agree to that?" He stared at me for a long moment before giving a little nod. "Okay. Can I trust you not to run away if I put you down, or should I carry you?"

Personally, I'd love to tote him around like my beautiful prize, but I wouldn't force him.

"I won't run."

I put him down and pointed into the distance. "My home is about half a mile this way." I started walking in that direction and was pleased when he stayed right by my side.

After several minutes of silence, my mate looked up at me and asked, "What's your name?"

"Stone."

"Like a rock?"

"I don't know of any other kind of stone," I replied with a smirk.

"I'm Wren; like the songbird."

"Is that a bullshit name?"

Wren's brows tucked in with anger. "I think it's a great name, thank you very much."

Another deep laugh rumbled in my chest. My mate seemed skittish, but I loved that he had a sassy side too. "Easy, songbird; I like the name. I was just asking if it was real; you sounded like you were hiding from someone, so I thought maybe you gave me a fake name."

"Oh." The anger melted from his face. "I didn't even think of that, but that's a good idea. It's too late now, I guess."

"I promise you're safe with me, Wren." Speaking his name caused my lips to tingle. My mate gave me the faintest of smiles, but it was breathtaking. What I told him was true; he was safer with me than anywhere else on the planet. I'd fight to protect him until my dying breath. He just didn't know it yet.

Chapter Three

Wren

My grip loosened on the knife Stone gave me as he led me through the woods and realization settled over me that he wasn't going to kill me. When I first saw him running at me, I was sure I was a goner; that he was a hired hitman sent to take me out.

He certainly looked the part; the man was *huge*. He was at least a foot taller than me and probably three times as broad. Add in his shaved head, chiseled jaw and scruffy face, and he made for an intimidating sight. He didn't look like any park ranger I'd ever seen, that's for damn sure.

But there was something about Stone that told me I could trust him. Maybe it was the kindness in his mossy green eyes, or the way his deep laugh made my stomach flip. Or maybe it was just the sharp blade he gave me, along with his permission to stab him. Whatever the reason, I felt safe by his side.

"Oh wow," I said as we entered a clearing which held three wooden cabins. "These homes are gorgeous."

"Thank you. I helped build them all," he replied proudly.

"Really? That's amazing."

He gave me a lopsided smile as he led me onto the porch of one of the buildings. "This one is mine."

"Who lives in the other two? More rangers?"

"Yeah, two rangers named Rowan and Phoenix, who happen to be my best friends." He opened his front door. "They live here with their...husbands."

"Aw, it's like you have your own cute little gay community here," I chuckled before panic seized my chest. *Oh god. I'm in the middle of the woods with a mountain man who just brought me back to his secluded land filled with other gay men. What if this is a gay cult? Is there such a thing?*

Apparently Stone saw the fear on my face, because he sighed and pulled another knife from a holster on his ankle that was hidden by his jeans. He offered me the weapon with the handle pointed towards me. "Do you trust me yet?"

"It depends," I answered as I gripped the handle. "How many more knives do you have hidden on you?"

Stone laughed a gravelly noise that warmed my stomach. "Three. Would you like them?"

I thought about it for a moment before waving him off. "No, that's okay. And

I'm sorry; you've been nothing but kind to me. My day has been seriously fucked up and I'm scared and shocked and I'm taking it out on you."

"It's okay," he told me seriously as he lifted his hand and patted my back with heavy thumps. It was equal parts touching and awkward. I got the feeling that Stone wasn't usually a nurturer, but he was making an effort for me and it was endearing as hell.

He waved me inside and I smiled when I saw his cabin's interior. There were no colors except for different shades of brown, and the only decor was several pairs of deer antlers hanging on the walls. It was masculine and rugged, and fit Stone well.

"Do you hunt?" I asked, pointing at the antlers.

"No. I found those while inspecting the area and thought they were pretty."

Hearing the word "pretty" come out of the big man's mouth put a goofy smile on my face. It was obvious that Stone had many layers under those delicious muscles of his. "They are," I agreed, and he smiled back.

"Do you want something to drink?"

"I'd love some water." I hadn't eaten or drank anything all day. Plus, I'd ran for miles so my throat was dry.

Stone went into his kitchen and retrieved a bottle of water from the fridge before sliding it across the counter to me. "I want you to tell me all about your fucked up day. I need to know who and what you're afraid of so I can keep you safe."

His words warmed me to my core; he barely knew me, but he wanted to protect me. He certainly appeared up to the task; he looked like he could tear Preston and his friends apart with his bare hands. But I didn't want to put him in danger. I wanted his insight and advice on the situation, but telling him my story could put both of us at risk.

"But that can wait until later if you want," Stone offered and I sighed in relief. "Right now we have other pressing matters to talk about."

"Like what?" I untwisted the cap from the bottle and took a big swig.

"Like the fact that I'm a wolf."

I nearly coughed up a lung as I choked on my water. "You're a *what*?"

"A wolf. Well, only half," he shrugged. "The other half is human, obviously."

Ohhh god. I'm stuck in the woods with a man who's hot as hell but nuttier than a squirrel turd. "So, you're saying you're...a werewolf?" As I asked, I picked my knives up from the counter and clutched them to my chest.

"Of course not." *Okay, maybe I misunderstood. Maybe this is some 'spirit animal' metaphor or something.*
"Werewolves are assholes. They're feral and run around biting people for sport. I'm a wolf shifter. I can change back and forth anytime I choose and I'm in control of my animal." *Yep, he's crazy.*

"You know, I'm not really that hungry," I lied as I crept backwards towards the door. "I think I'll just be on my way."

"If I show you my wolf, will you believe me?"

"I think I'd have to, right?" *What the hell, Wren? Why are you calling his bluff? Just run!* But before I got my feet in gear, my head went stupid when Stone pulled off his shirt and I got an uninhibited view of his body. Good god, he was gorgeous. His chest and stomach were smooth and ripped to hell. They, along with his arms, looked like they had watermelons stuffed under their skin. "Um, what are you doing?" I asked when I could form speech.

"I don't want to rip my clothes when I shift."

"Right." I swallowed hard when Stone kicked off his boots and pulled down his jeans and boxers. His thighs looked as thick as tree trunks. I couldn't see the good parts because he was bent over. *Damn, I wish he wasn't a fruit loop because he's the sexiest man I've ever seen.*

I cringed when the sound of breaking bones pierced the air. Stone's back arched as he got on all fours. His large hands turned to paws with claws and hair, and his face morphed into a snout. A tail grew from the base of his spine and thick, gray fur sprouted all over his body until Stone was no longer in front of me. There was only a wolf, which slinked around the kitchen counter and pawed towards me.

"Holy shit!" I threw both of my knives at the creature, and one embedded into each of its shoulders. The wolf rolled its eyes at me - hand to god, *rolled its eyes* before its fur sucked back into its skin and its body morphed and snapped until Stone returned.

"Man, that stings like a bitch," he said as he gripped the knife handles and pulled the blades from his flesh. I watched in awe as the wounds shrank and closed, not even leaving a scar behind.

"My god, you really are what you said you were." I placed both of my trembling hands to my face. "You...you just turned into a wolf."

"I warned you."

"A person can't prepare for something like that!" I braced myself against the kitchen counter and took several slow deep breaths to keep from passing out from shock. "Why did your wounds heal so quickly?" Of all the questions I had, that one popped out first.

"Shifters are different than humans."

"You don't say."

Stone gave a booming laugh. "No, I mean we have different properties. We're very hard to injure and we heal quickly. We're fast, strong, and immune to disease. We can be killed, but we're naturally immortal."

Of course he's immortal. Why wouldn't *he be immortal?* My knees went weak as I thought about everything I just saw and heard. "I think I need to sit down."

Stone led me over to his sofa and helped me sit down. When I did, I was eye level with his cock, which was rock solid and *huge*. The uncut monster could probably cover the area between my elbow and wrist. I almost held my arm out to measure.

"Like what you see?" Stone asked in a husky yet teasing tone.

"I'm so sorry for staring," I told him, though I made no effort to move my gaze.

"Don't be sorry; I *want* you to look at me. You're my mate."

That pulled my eyes away and up to his face. "I'm your what now?"

"My mate. Have you heard that some animals mate for life?" I nodded slowly. "It's the same with shifters. We have one mate whom we love, provide for and protect our whole lives, which, as I told you, are immortal. Unlike animals, our mate is chosen for us by Fate. She picks our perfect match in every way, and we recognize them by scent and instinct when we meet them."

"And you recognized me," I surmised.

"Yes." I nodded again, because what the hell could I say to that? "And you don't have to worry about being human," Stone continued, "Because when we bond, you'll inherit my immortal life. You'll also heal faster than normal if you get injured."

You'll inherit my immortal life. That was a sentence I didn't plan on ever hearing. "And how do we bond?" I knew I'd probably regret the question as it left my lips.

"I fuck you and bite your neck."

Why I nearly dropped my pants and said 'Let's go!' was beyond my comprehension. Luckily, my shock over the situation and my trepidation about the size of his dick reigned me back in.

"That will bind us together forever," Stone added. "And just so you know, now that I've met you, I can never get aroused by anyone but you. You are the only person I want. You have all of my attention and desire."

The fact that this sexy adonis was aroused by little ol' me sent my heart racing...but then guilt ballooned in my gut. "And that doesn't bother you?" Stone gave me a confused look. "You look young. What are you...thirty five? Thirty seven? You still have a *lot* of life to live, and there's tons of guys out there. You're not disappointed to be stuck with me forever just because you sniffed me?"

"First of all, I'm eighty two," he countered, and my eyes widened. He looked great for an old geezer. "And don't worry about me missing out; I've been around the block a time or two with plenty of men."

Wait a minute. "Exactly how many men are we talking about here?" I asked, crossing my arms. *Am I jealous? Why am I jealous?*

He gave me a knowing smirk. "You don't have to worry about my past, songbird. I promise it meant nothing."

The nickname turned my insides to goo, but I pushed the feeling away. "What if *I* don't want to miss out?" I'd had exactly one boyfriend and look how that turned out. Still, as I said the words, they left a sour taste in my mouth.

Stone's face fell and his huge dick slowly deflated. Even soft, it was impressive. He took a seat beside me and stared at the floor. "You're human, so things are different for you. Our meeting won't prohibit you from desiring someone else. You'll feel the mate pull between us; you'll miss me when we're apart and may even get sick if it's for a long period of time, and it will get stronger the longer we're together. Once we've bonded, the idea of being with someone else will turn your stomach."

He scrubbed a hand over his slick scalp and added, "But if there's something you need to experience before you're ready to bond, it will tear me apart, but I understand. Forever is a long time for regrets."

I wished I could take back my question because his reaction to it was tearing *me* apart. He forced a smile as he looked at me, but I could see the pain in his eyes. It hurt to see the big man so upset, which confused the hell out of me. I'd just met him. It was surely the mate pull he talked about, but seeing as I'd known about mates for all of five minutes, that was also making my brain spin. Plus there was the whole *I saw someone get fucking murdered earlier* thing putting me on edge. Everything was too much to process. I needed to step away from Stone and get my head straight.

"Would it be okay if I took that shower now?"

"Sure."

He stood from the sofa and motioned for me to follow him. He either forgot or didn't care that he was still naked. *I* sure as hell didn't care; his ass looked like two perfectly round hams that I wanted to sink my teeth into. *Wait, am I horny or hungry?* I shrugged and decided I was both as Stone led me into the bathroom.

"There are fresh towels in the closet and I'll put some clean clothes on the sink once you're in the shower. Take your time."

"Thank you."

He gave me a tight smile and nod before leaving me alone in the room that was decorated in (shocker) more brown. I folded Stone's coat neatly and placed it on the sink, but threw the rest of my clothes in every direction before twisting the shower knobs and stepping into the basin.

The cold January weather had me frozen to the core, but the hot water raining over me felt like heaven. I slowly regained feeling in my toes and my skin turned pink from the heat. Stone's body wash smelled like coconut and turned the steamy room into my own private oasis.

I heard Stone enter the room as I scrubbed my body, but he didn't speak. He was probably giving me time to sort through everything he told me, which I was grateful for. He'd dumped a *lot* of information on me; information I never would have believed if I didn't see Stone in his wolf form. I still didn't understand how such a thing was possible. The longer I thought about it, the more questions I came up with. Once I was clean and warm, I'd ask Stone to explain it all to me.

The part that kept creeping to the forefront of my mind was what he said about mates. The idea of having one special person to share forever with was beautiful, and admittedly something I wanted. But I knew very little about my "eternal mate"; just that he was kind to offer me his home and food (not to mention the coat right off of his back), honest because of the way he told me so openly about his identity, good with his hands because he built his own home, sexy as hell and hung like a horse. *Huh. I guess I know more than I thought.* I also knew that he was happy to have me in his home and as his partner, which warmed my heart.

Still, the past twelve hours had completely turned my world on its head. *I'm on the run from my murderous ex-boyfriend who wants me dead, only to find my fated magical wolf boyfriend who wants to bite my neck and turn me immortal. How is this my life?*

Chapter Four

Stone

I sighed as I stepped back into my clothes. *I think I blew it with my mate.* Subtlety had never been my strong suit; I was a 'rip the bandage off' kind of guy. I wanted to be honest with Wren without hiding anything, but I should have been more delicate about the way I told him about myself. Delicacy wasn't my strong suit either. I was just so excited to meet Wren and have him in my home that I blurted out everything and completely overwhelmed him.

But the real kick in the balls was the way he reacted when he heard about mates; about being *my* mate. He didn't seem happy or excited or interested at all, really. Sure, he stared at my dick, but let's be honest, it's impressive. I've got ten inches of fat meat between my legs; who *wouldn't* stare?

But all he seemed concerned about was not wanting to miss out on things with other men; about being tied down to me forever. I wanted to throw the coffee table into the wall and demand he stay away from any other male, but that probably would have sent the wrong message. I didn't hate Wren for having interest in others; I could never hate my mate. I hated every other man on Earth for *having* his interest. I didn't want him to get the two confused.

So, I told him the words that turned my stomach and shredded my soul; that I understood if he needed to 'play the field' before our bonding. I'd done enough of that myself and knew it could mean nothing. Wren looked young and maybe he wasn't quite ready to settle down yet. I'd wait for him. If he had to fuck every other man in town to be ready to spend forever with me, it would kill me, but I only wanted his happiness. I'd do anything for him, even if it destroyed me.

But then a brilliant idea popped into my head; maybe there was a way for us both to win. I needed to show him how great having a mate could be; that it was more than an eternity of sizzling sex. You could have sex with anyone, but mates had a special connection. I needed to romance the shit out of him so that he didn't even think about another man; to show him I was his perfect match.

It was brilliant in theory, but the problem would be in the execution. I didn't know a thing about romance. I'd never had to romance a man in my life. When I visited the club in town, all I had to do was take off my shirt and make my pecs dance and men fell to their knees. But my Wren deserved better than that.

Then I got another brilliant idea. *I'm on a roll.* My pack knew all about love and glitter and pancakes and all kinds of mushy shit. Surely they could teach me something. Tonight I needed to find out what Wren was running from and make sure he was safe and comfortable, but I'd call the pack over in the morning for tips.

I nodded in agreement with myself and wandered over to the fridge to pull out a large pot of vegetable soup. It was fresh from lunchtime and I could heat it up quickly for Wren. It wasn't the fanciest dinner, but it would fill him up and stick to his ribs.

Just as the soup came to a boil, Wren emerged from the bathroom and my jaw dropped. He was even more beautiful than I remembered. His wet hair was combed back from his forehead, making his blue eyes pop even more. He was dressed in the clothes I laid out for him; one of my plain white t-shirts and a pair of my gray sleep pants. The shirt hung to his knees and there was a big lump beneath it where he'd tied the waist of the pants in a knot to keep them up.

God, he's sexy. Ooh, I should tell him that. Wait, is that romantic? Should I say something else? Maybe I should tell him he's handsome. But that sounds kind of corny.

"Does it hurt?" Wren asked, interrupting my thoughts and chasing away my opportunity to be romantic.

"Does what hurt?"

"When you turn into a wolf. It looked painful."

"Oh." His question surprised me, but I was thrilled at his interest. "No. It feels like a big stretch after a nap." I turned off the stove burner and grabbed two bowls out of the cabinet.

"Huh. So did something turn you into a shifter?"

"Nah. It's not like werewolves getting turned by a bite or anything like that. Shifters are their own species that have been around since the beginning of time. We're born this way."

"So if you were to bite me, I wouldn't become a wolf?"

My pulse pounded with the knowledge that he'd at least thought about our bonding. "No. Like I said earlier, you'd inherit a few of my properties, but you'd stay human."

"Why don't people know about shifters?"

"People can be dicks," I shrugged, making Wren snort a laugh. "Shifters are large and strong by nature. In the past, humans feared us because of our stature and our animal side. They claimed we were 'capable of great violence'. Well, spoiler alert, *anyone* is capable of great violence. There are good and bad shifters like there are good and bad humans. But just because we look the part and there have been some asshole shifters that caused destruction, people assume the worst of us. We've been hunted in the past, so we tend to keep our true identity to ourselves."

"Shifters are kind of like Pit Bulls," Wren answered thoughtfully. I had my back turned to him as I filled our bowls with soup, and gave him a confused look over my shoulder. "The whole breed gets a bad reputation because of the violence of a few. But I've met lots of Pit Bulls who were sweet as pie." I laughed as I shook my head. The man was precious. "I'm sorry that I was scared of you when I first saw you. I mean, I didn't know you were a shifter, but I did kind of judge you on your size."

I grabbed our bowls and gave him an understanding smile as I turned to face him. "You were also terrified *before* I came barging into the clearing, so I'm sure that didn't help." Besides that, I knew I was an intimidating sight to say the least. It went a long way in protecting my pack; people didn't want to start trouble with the big, scary guy. But I never wanted to scare Wren. "Come on, let's sit down. You need to eat."

I shuffled behind Wren as he walked over to my dining table on the other side of the room. He put his hand on the back of the chair but when I yelled, "Stop!", he dropped his hand immediately and looked at me with huge eyes. *Shit.* "Sorry." I placed our bowls on the table and stepped next to him. "I just wanted to..." I pulled his chair out from under the table for him. It was something I'd seen both Phoenix and Rowan do countless times for their mates.

Wren gave me a shy smile and touched his hand to my arm, sending a shudder down my spine. "Thank you." Once he was seated and I pushed him closer to the table, I collected two spoons and two bottles of water before sitting next to him.

"Thank you for *all* of this," Wren continued. "For the food and the shower and the clothes. I don't think I've said that yet and I should have. I really appreciate this. Without you, I'd still be freezing in the woods."

"You're welcome." I took a chance and cupped his smooth cheek in my hand. He didn't flinch and even gave me another heartstopping smile. I didn't want to press my luck, so I pulled my hand away after only a moment. "Will you tell me *why* you were in the woods?"

Wren sighed and nodded, dropping his gaze to his soup as he stirred it. "You already guessed that I'm hiding from someone. That someone is my boy...well, *ex*-boyfriend Preston." My insides burned with jealousy at the thought of Wren having a relationship with someone else, but I tried my best to keep it hidden, and just nodded for him to continue his story.

"This afternoon I went to his house and walked in on something I shouldn't have. I saw him kill a man." *Wait, is that it?* I'd killed lots of people (granted it was out of necessity and protection), but I knew enough not to say that out loud and scare Wren even more. "In cold blood," he continued, looking at me like he was waiting for a reaction.

"Are you okay?" Even though I was used to this sort of thing, I could tell sweet Wren was bothered deeply.

"I think so. It happened so fast. And it was nothing like the movies; just a quick pop of the gun and he was gone." I placed my hand on his shoulder in support and he gave me a half smile in appreciation. "When I was running through the woods, I couldn't stop thinking about it. The man probably had family and friends." He dropped his gaze to the table when he said, "I didn't know him, but I mourned for him. I had to stop running because I was crying so hard. I cried for him for an hour and said a little prayer. I don't know if it will help him, but...just in case, you know?" I nodded and squeezed his shoulder. My mate was too pure for this world.

Wren suffered a traumatic event, but he seemed to be moving on. *So why was he running? Why is he still scared? There has to be more to the story.* Wren looked at me again and added, "And now Preston wants to keep me quiet by killing me too."

"That son of a bitch!" I roared, slamming my fist into the table. Wren's eyes grew wide again. "I'm sorry," I offered as I reigned myself in. "The thought of someone wanting to harm you infuriates me."

Wren smiled sweetly again and ducked his head before continuing, "Anyway, he's a police officer, so I can't go to the cops. He knows where I live, so I can't go home. *And* he knows where I work, so I can't go back to my job. I didn't know what else to do, so I just ran. I know he's out looking for me and I'm terrified."

I dropped my hand from Wren's shoulder to take his. He didn't pull away, and even squeezed my palm in return. "You don't have to be afraid. I'll protect you with everything that I am. So will my pack."

"Your pack?" he asked, cocking his head.

"My wolf pack," I smiled. "Phoenix and Rowan, the rangers I mentioned earlier, are shifters too. Phoenix is the leader of our pack, which consists of him, his mate Rory, and Rowan and his mate Dax. And me, of course."

"Rory and Dax aren't shifters?"

"No, they're human like you. They joined our pack after bonding with their mates, but we'll *all* look after you. I won't let anything happen to you, songbird."

"Thank you," he whispered, squeezing my hand even tighter.

"And in case I didn't make it clear, I want you to stay here with me. You'll be safe here. Plus, I just...you know...want you with me." *Holy hell, I suck at this.* "If you want to stay with me, that is." He didn't have much of an option, but I'd never *make* him stay.

"I do." He smiled at me again and my heart damn near beat right out of my chest. This little blond beauty had me wrapped around his finger and he didn't even know it.

Wren and I held hands as we finished our meal. I'd never just sat and held a man's hand, and was surprised at how amazing it felt. Of course, it only felt amazing because it was with my mate. But as wonderful as it was, it was also a little challenging. Holding onto Wren meant I had to eat with my left hand, which was pretty useless. It shook and dribbled and irritated the hell out of me until I just put my spoon down and watched Wren eat instead. I smiled as he gobbled up every bite and scraped the bottom of his bowl.

"Would you like some more?"

"Yes, please," he said as his cheeks tinged pink.

"Hey, there's no judgement from this corner. Trust me, I'm a big eater too." I regrettably let go of him to refill his bowl from the pot on the stove. When I returned, Wren's brows were tucked in.

"But you didn't even finish yours."

"Oh, um..." I wasn't sure of a non-pathetic way to tell him '*I didn't eat mine because I love holding your hand and my left arm is stupid'.* But I didn't have to tell him anything. I saw the moment of recognition in Wren's eyes, and the way his cheeks glowed deeper red as he pursed his lips to keep from smiling. He didn't say anything, but he did move his hand onto my knee so that I could eat freely. What he didn't know was that I was rock hard under the table from just that simple touch.

"Can I help you with the dishes?" he asked once we'd both destroyed two bowls full of soup.

"That's okay. I'll just rinse them out and leave them for tomorrow."

"I want to help," he countered. "You've done so much for me; it's the least I can do."

I didn't want Wren to have to lift a finger, but I could see this was important to him. So, we went to the sink together. He scrubbed the dishes and I dried them and put them away. It was a little thing, but it felt nice. We were a great team and I enjoyed doing something couple-y with him. When Wren dried his hands on the dish towel, his lips stretched into a wide yawn.

"Are you ready for bed?"

He nodded and rubbed at his eyes. "I'm usually a night owl, but I'm exhausted from all that running today."

"I'll show you to my bedroom." I didn't miss the way Wren's eyes widened slightly with panic. I didn't want to do anything to overwhelm him or make him uncomfortable. "The bed is all yours; I'll sleep on the couch."

"I don't want to steal your bed. *I'll* take the couch."

There was no way in hell I was letting my mate sleep on the sofa while I took the only bed in the house. "You're not stealing it; I'm giving it to you."

Wren gave me a frustrated huff. "You can't sleep on the sofa; you're way too tall."

"Then I'll sleep on the floor," I shrugged.

"There's no way you'll be comfortable there."

"I will be if I'm in wolf form." There was another flash of panic in his eyes. "Remember, I'm in complete control of my animal. It's me, just furry."

Wren nodded slowly. He could probably tell there was no arguing with me about this. "If you're sure you'll be comfortable."

"I am. Follow me."

After a quick stop in the bathroom to brush our teeth together (another couple-y thing that made my heart race), I led Wren into my bedroom. Like the rest of the house, it was simple and clean, and held only the necessary furniture, including the California King size bed covered in a thick brown duvet.

"Comfy?" I asked once Wren burrowed under the covers.

"Oh my god, this is the best mattress I've ever been on. And look at this!" He stretched his arms over his head and pointed his toes. "I can't reach either end. This thing is huge!"

I chuckled at his excitement and tucked the blankets tightly around him. "I'm glad you like it." As far as I was concerned, this would be his bed until we wore it out with our lovemaking and had to buy a new one, which I'd obviously let Wren choose. "I'm going to shift now." I gave him a teasing smile and added, "Try not to stab me this time, okay?"

"No promises," he teased back with a smirk. *Damn, he's perfect.*

As I stepped out of my clothes, I could actually feel Wren's gaze upon me and I smelled his arousal in the air. Now that he wasn't scared out of his skull, my mate's body was reacting to seeing mine. Against every ounce of my instincts, I kept my back turned to him so that he wouldn't see how he affected me; I didn't want him to think I expected something that he wasn't ready to give.

I transitioned into wolf form and turned around to face my mate again. He still looked a little nervous of my animal, judging by the way he gripped the blanket tightly in his hands.

"Stone?" he asked in a quiet voice. I lowered my head to show him that I wasn't a threat, and that he didn't have to be afraid. "It's you, just furry," he repeated, as if trying to convince himself.

I crept slowly towards him, keeping my head low and my ears tucked back. When I reached the bed, Wren scooted to the edge of the mattress and stared at me in silence for a couple of minutes. Finally, a smile slowly crossed his lips.

"I can tell it's you," he whispered. "Because of your eyes. You have beautiful eyes, Stone." Wren laughed when my tail whipped from side to side. I couldn't help it; he made me so damn happy I couldn't hold it in. The sound of his laughter just made it wag that much harder; it was soft, soothing and melodious. *He really* is *my songbird.*

"You're not so scary, are you? You're just a big ol' sweetie." Wren lifted his hand but stopped shy of touching my head. "Can I pet you? That's not weird, is it?" I chuffed a laugh and nudged his hand with my nose. Wren ran his fingers over my head and scratched behind my ears. He pet me in long strokes down my back and laughed again when my tail thumped against the wood floor. "Thank you," he told me when he pulled his hand away.

I wanted to thank him too, so I put my paws on the edge of the bed and licked his cheek. Wren flinched and looked at me wide-eyed again. *Shit, was that too far? I went too far.*

"Does that count as our first kiss?" he asked before erupting into giggles. The sound stole my heart, though it was already his. "I guess I should give you one too." He pursed his lips and pressed a kiss to my cold, wet nose, then his own nose crinkled when he yawned widely. "Thank you again for everything. Goodnight, Stone."

I watched as he nestled his head onto the pillow and pulled the blankets up to his chin. I walked in a circle a few times before lying down on the most comfortable spot on the floor. I closed my eyes but they popped open again when I felt a presence on my back, when Wren gently stroked through my fur. He pet me slowly and lazily until his hand stopped and his breathing evened out. Once I was sure he was asleep, I nudged his hand back up onto the mattress. As much as I wanted his touch, I didn't want his arm to get sore through the night. I once again closed my eyes and drifted off to dreams of my beautiful mate.

Chapter Five

Stone

I peeled my eyes open and stretched my paws out in front of me. It'd been a long time since I spent a whole night in wolf form. After a big yawn, I noticed my back was warm and there was a comforting weight on my side. I looked over my shoulder and found Wren lying on the floor with me, snuggled into my back, sleeping soundly with his hand buried in my fur.

Oh, songbird. I wondered what brought him down there with me; whether he was cold or lonely or scared. Whatever the reason, I was thrilled he came to me for comfort. I just wished he would have woken me up so that I could have held him or talked him through whatever was bothering him. Or tried to, anyway. Maybe I wasn't the best at words or emotions, but I'd do anything for my mate.

I scooted away from Wren without waking him before I shifted into human form. I gently scooped him into my arms and settled him back onto the bed, tucking the blankets around him. I grinned from ear to ear when he whispered my name in his sleep and burrowed further into the mattress.

I stepped into a pair of sweatpants and a t-shirt, tiptoed out into the kitchen, grabbed my landline phone from the wall and dialed Phoenix's number. I could have walked over to his home, but I didn't want to leave Wren alone.

"Hello?" the alpha answered groggily.

"I need you and Rory to come over. It's an emergency."

"What's wrong?" Now his voice was clear and focused.

"It's a good emergency," I replied quickly so I wouldn't startle him. "I found my mate."

"Holy shit."

"Who is it?" Rory's sleepy voice asked in the background.

"It's Stone. He found his mate." There was a loud squeal followed by a rustling noise over the line.

"Tell. Me. Everything," Rory demanded when he stole the phone.

"Come over and I will. Bring Rowan and Dax, too." I snorted when the call went dead. Rory was too excited to even say goodbye.

I pulled three dozen eggs and two pounds of bacon out of my fridge, and pans from my cabinets. I knew my pack would be hungry, and thought it'd be nice for them to meet Wren over breakfast. I had good ideas every once in a while.

I barely had the eggs whisked together when my door burst open and Phoenix, Rory, Rowan and Dax shoved their way inside my cabin. Rory plastered both of his hands on the opposite side of the counter and looked me square in the face.

"Okay, we're here. Spill it." He had a wicked case of bedhead and Dax's flannel shirt was buttoned crooked. They'd obviously come over in a hurry.

"Good morning to you too," I replied with a smirk.

"Hold on, is that bacon?" Dax asked, eyeballing the sizzling skillet. Rowan's pleasantly plump mate sniffed the air and smiled. "Mm, gossip *and* food. It doesn't get better than this."

"Thank you for cooking," Rowan offered as he wrapped his arm around his man. "I didn't have a chance to make anything for Dax yet."

"I'm not just cooking for you." I stood up straight and announced proudly, "I'm also making breakfast for my mate."

Phoenix's eyes widened. "He's *here*?"

"He's still asleep in my bed."

Dax's smile spread. "You dirty dog."

"It's not like that. I *can* meet a man and not fuck his brains out, you know." The four of them stared back in shock and I just rolled my eyes before pouring the eggs into the empty pan.

"Okay, I need details like yesterday," Rory insisted. The man looked ready to burst with curiosity.

"Start making some toast and we'll talk." I snorted a laugh at how quickly he jogged around the counter to the toaster, and again at the way Phoenix followed him closely, grabbing butter and jelly out of the fridge to help.

I told the group all about how I met Wren hiding in the forest, what he told me about his ex-boyfriend, and bringing him back to my place.

"That poor man," Dax said sadly as Rowan pulled him closer.

"I know. My songbird has been through a lot."

Rory gasped. "Did you just call him songbird?"

"Yeeaaah," I drawled, wondering what he was getting at.

He punched his hand in the air and turned to Phoenix. "Pay up, babe."

Phoenix looked as confused as I felt. "What are you talking about?"

"Our bet! Remember? Row, Dax and I all bet you ten bucks that Stone would give his mate a cutesy nickname. 'Songbird' is adorable, so cough it up."

"Damn." Dax and Rowan gave a high five as Phoenix dug out his wallet. "Wait." The alpha turned to me. "Have you actually called him that to his face?" I nodded. "Damn," he repeated as he passed out three ten dollar bills to the pack. Dax and Rowan snickered as they stuffed their money in their pockets, while Rory blew his man a kiss.

"So what does songbird look like?" Rory asked curiously.

"First of all, only *I* get to call him that." Phoenix gave me a warning glare for my tone while Rory just laughed as he buttered some toast. "And secondly, he's fucking gorgeous. He's small and thin with light blond hair and his eyes are the deepest blue I've ever seen."

"Oh my god, you're so in love," Dax teased.

"Well of course I am. He's my mate and he's perfect."

"Have you told him that yet?" Rowan asked.

"That I love him? No. That he's my mate? Yes."

Rory spun around and stared at me with giant eyes. "He was in shock after seeing a guy get whacked and you dropped the wolf bomb on him?"

"I didn't know he'd seen a guy get whacked when I told him," I defended. "Besides, he stabbed me so we're even."

"Sweet jesus, I can't wait to meet this guy," Dax beamed.

"Look, after the stabbing, he took everything really well. And I'm glad I told him; his ex obviously hid a lot from him, and I refuse to do that. I want him to feel safe with me, and I think I need to be honest with him for that to happen."

"I agree," Phoenix told me with a gentle smile. "You did the right thing."

"So, is he accepting of everything?" Rowan piped up.

"He likes my wolf. He um...he pet me." I was worried my friends may find that odd, but Phoenix and Rowan smiled while the other two gave a simultaneous *'awww'*.

"I'm not so sure about the bonding part. We didn't talk about it much." I was too embarrassed to mention that Wren may be interested in other men.

"Don't worry," Rory instructed with a thump on my shoulder. "We'll talk you up and help him see how great you are."

"Thank you," I told him seriously. "Could you help me with one more thing as well? It's a big reason why I called you over."

"Name it," Phoenix requested.

"I need pointers on how to be..." I turned my attention to the stovetop, too self-conscious to look at any of them when I concluded, "Romantic."

"How you described Wren to us was pretty damn romantic," Dax answered. I was grateful none of them laughed at me. "Did you tell him how attractive you find him?"

"I..." I thought back over the night's events and my stomach dropped. I certainly *thought* the words, but I didn't actually speak them. "Fuck."

"You *have* to compliment him," Rory insisted. "Especially after what he's been through, he needs to be built up and made to feel special."

"Flowers are a nice touch," Rowan added.

"So are backrubs," Dax chimed in. As soon as he spoke, Rowan stepped behind him and kneaded his lover's shoulders. *Dick. Whipped.*

Phoenix just smiled at the scene. "And I'd say you're on the right track by preparing him breakfast."

"Compliments, flowers, massages and food," I repeated. "I think I can handle that."

"Great. So what are you planning on doing together today?" Rowan asked curiously.

"I don't know. I thought I might show him some moves this afternoon."

"Moves?" Dax asked, arching an eyebrow.

"You know...defense moves. Well, *and* offensive ones. Fighting in general."

"Oh good lord." Dax pinched the bridge of his nose. "You're trying to be romantic, so you thought punching the hell out of each other was a good idea? It's a good thing you called us." I personally didn't see the problem, but I guess that's why I needed help.

"Ooh, we're watching rom-coms tonight to gear up for Valentine's Day," Rory interrupted excitedly. "Why don't you come over and watch them with us? They're sweet and gooey and will give you more romantic ideas."

"That sounds terrible," I grumbled as I scraped the scrambled eggs onto a platter.

"Fine then, we'll invite Wren," Dax shrugged. "If he accepts, I bet you'll come over with him."

"Of course I will. I'll suffer through anything that makes him happy."

"Aww," the group cooed in unison, making me roll my eyes again.

"Just set the table, will you? I'm going to go wake him up."

I lumbered down the hall towards my bedroom with an odd feeling in my stomach; it was jittery with excitement over seeing Wren again, even though we'd only been apart a few minutes. I couldn't wait to show him off to my pack. *Dax is right; I'm so in love.*

*****

Wren

I stretched and reached out to bury my hand in Stone's wiry fur, but only got a fist full of blankets. I opened my eyes and sat bolt upright, looking for Stone, but I was alone in his dark room. Equal parts fear and longing filled me up; I had an indescribable, desperate need to be with him, so I jumped from bed and jogged out of the room. I barely made it into the hallway when I ran face first into his broad, firm chest.

"Stone." I wrapped my arms around his thick waist and squeezed him for all I was worth. After tensing for a moment, he hugged me back and rested his cheek on the top of my head.

"Are you alright?"

"Yeah. I woke up and you were gone and I...I guess I panicked." *Wow, that sounds pathetic out loud.*

"I'm sorry I left you alone. I just came out to make breakfast." I sniffed the air, catching the savory aroma of bacon. It wasn't until that moment that I realized how hungry I was. "I was coming to wake you up."

His words brought about a realization; the last I remembered, I was on the floor snuggled up to Stone, and when I woke up, I was alone in his bed. And there was only one way for me to have gotten there; he must have wanted space. *Shit.* "I'm sorry if I crossed a line last night." Stone pulled back to give me a confused look.

"When I laid down with you," I explained. "I had a dream about seeing Mick get shot and it really bothered me." *Okay, this isn't sounding any less pathetic.* "I needed you and came down to be next to you and I guess I fell asleep. I'm sorry."

Stone's confusion melted into an understanding smile. "Don't be sorry. I love having you close to me. I only moved you back onto the bed so you'd be comfortable while I cooked." He moved his hand from around me to pat my cheek in a clumsily adorable gesture. "I always want to be near you, songbird." His words sent my heart into overdrive and made my knees weak.

When a loud, "Aww," sounded from the direction of the kitchen, I flinched and attached myself to Stone again.

"It's okay; that's just my pack being...well, my pack."

"The other wolf men are here?" I asked the question quietly, but still heard snickering in return.

"They really want to meet you."

The fact that Stone already told his friends about me made my heart squeeze; it was like he was proud to introduce me to them. But I was nervous about what they may think of me. Stone didn't seem to mind that I was a wimpy little wisp, but what if the others were pissed that they had to look out for me? What if they decided I wasn't worth the trouble?

It was then I realized that I was still dressed in Stone's clothing, which bagged off of me and only emphasized my small stature. Not to mention that they were wrinkled and disheveled from sleep. "I can't meet them like this," I whispered. "I look terrible."

"You look beautiful," Stone countered, and butterflies took flight in my stomach. I thought he was attracted to me, given that he said his desire was all for me (plus that hard monster cock he was sporting), but to hear the words was better than I could have imagined. "You're so beautiful, Wren."

"Yes!" sounded from the kitchen, followed by the noise of a hand slapping another in a high-five.

"It sounds like you have your own cheering section in there."

Stone gave an irritated glance over his shoulder before looking back at me. "I'm sorry about them. There aren't many boundaries between packmates." He leaned in close to my ear and added, "If you're not comfortable meeting them, I'll kick them out."

Having Stone toss his friends out on their asses was surely not the way to give them warm and fuzzy feelings about me. "No, I'd like to meet them." I couldn't put it off forever and besides, these men were important to Stone. If he and I were going to have a relationship, I had to make an effort with his friends. Plus, I was really hungry and wanted that bacon.

"Thank you." He pressed a kiss to my cheek and my breath caught in my chest. He wrapped his arm around me and my feet practically floated off of the floor as he led me into the kitchen. They slammed back onto solid ground when I rounded the corner and found four men staring back at me.

The first to his feet was a man who was about as tall as Stone. He was nowhere near as broad, but I could tell he was obviously strong by the way his muscles shifted beneath his clothing as he approached me. With each step he took towards me, I took a half step back until my spine was flush with Stone's stomach and I couldn't go any farther.

"Hello, Wren," the man greeted with a kind smile that lit up his emerald green eyes. "My name is Phoenix." He wrapped his large hand around my small one and shook it gently.

"Stone told me you were the leader," I blurted out dumbly. My cheeks heated, but Phoenix just smiled wider.

"Yes, I'm the alpha of the Pine Ridge Pack. I lead our small pack alongside my mate Rory."

I blinked in surprise when Rory stepped out from behind his mate; he was only a few inches taller and a little thicker than me. He gave off a nerdy chic vibe with his bedhead, chunky glasses and pearly grin. "It's nice to meet you, Wren."

"You too." I was grateful for another man around my size; especially when he looked as friendly as Rory.

As if he read my thoughts, Rory leaned in closer and said quietly, "I know these guys can be a little intimidating, but trust me; when it comes to their mates and friends, they're just big teddy bears." I chuckled as he winked and waved over a cute, thickset man with a scruffy auburn beard and eyes that squinted into little slits as he smiled. "This is my best friend Dax." I shook Dax's hand and we exchanged pleasantries as well.

"And last but not least, this is my mate Rowan," Dax announced proudly.

The fourth and final man stepped forward to shake my hand before wrapping his arm around his man. Rowan was tall and strong like the other shifters, and had pretty ice blue eyes. All four of the men were handsome, but nobody could compare to Stone. I was convinced that he was the most gorgeous man on the planet. He could call it the mate pull all he wanted, but I just called it fact.

"Let's eat before the food gets cold," Stone suggested.

I smiled as the shifters (including Stone) pulled out chairs for their mates.

Then I watched in awe as they each piled a plate high with eggs, bacon and toast before placing it in front of their partner. Rory was right; they *were* just big teddy bears, who obviously loved doting on their mates. *I could get used to this.*

"Thank you," I told Stone as he positioned my plate on the table. After a quick peek around to make sure no one was watching, I pressed a kiss to his cheek. I thought his face would crack from how widely he grinned in response.

"Would you like orange juice or milk?"

"Orange juice sounds great, but I can get...it." Stone was already halfway across the kitchen before I finished my sentence. He returned a moment later with two full glasses. "Thank you." He crowded into my space and I knew what he wanted. I kissed his cheek again and that beautiful smile returned. My big man was eating every tender gesture up with a spoon and I loved it.

"Stone told us a little about your ordeal," Rowan started after we'd all tucked into our breakfast. "I'm so sorry you had to go through that."

"Thanks." I washed a bite down with a gulp of orange juice. "I didn't know Preston long, but I never would've thought he was capable of doing something like that."

"Do you know *why* he did it?" Phoenix questioned.

It was then that I realized how little I'd told Stone about what I witnessed. So, I recounted every detail of the event; everything I heard and saw, along with my assumptions of bribes or dirty money.

"Greed can make men do terrible things," the alpha responded sadly. "It can turn them against their friends and family."

Rory took his hand and Phoenix gave his mate a grateful smile. It seemed to be an act of comfort and though it was none of my business, I couldn't stop my curiosity.

"Did something happen to you too?"

Phoenix nodded. "It's important that you know our pack's history, but it's not a pleasant one. I know you've been through a lot; is it okay if I tell you now?" I could see why Phoenix was the leader; he was direct but not pushy, and was thoughtful of other people's needs and emotions. He seemed to have a level head and a firm foundation. Stone was undoubtedly the muscle of the group; the protector. I wasn't sure of Rowan's role just yet, but I hoped to learn more about him soon.

I reached for Stone's hand under the table, needing the support of his touch. The moment his big palm encased mine, soothing peace washed over me and I was confident I could handle whatever Phoenix needed to tell me. I squeezed Stone's hand and gave the alpha a nod to continue.

"Many years ago, my brother Raven killed my parents, who were the alpha and alpha-mate of the Silver Birch Pack," he began, and I gasped. I wasn't expecting something so sinister straight away. "He was born an alpha like me, but instead of following his destiny and building his own pack, he became greedy for what my father already owned. Raven challenged him for his pack, but my father refused to fight his son and was struck down in cold blood. I fled my homeland with Rowan and Stone, and we formed our own pack here. We built our homes with our own hands and are the caretakers for this land."

"Several months ago, Raven resurfaced. His followers were dwindling, and he was left with only a dozen men who were as wicked and bloodthirsty as he was. I don't know if it was greed, pride, or a final act of bravado, but he challenged me to a fight to the death. I didn't want to fight him, but I had no choice; if I forfeited, he would have taken our homes, my pack...and my mate." He leaned over to kiss Rory's forehead and I could actually feel his heartache over the possibility.

"While Raven and I battled, his pack viciously attacked mine. We *all* had to fight for our lives that day, but we prevailed and now the Silver Birch Pack will never bother us again."

It wasn't hard to draw a conclusion to what he meant; they killed all of the men in the other pack. But that knowledge didn't scare or anger me. Unlike Preston or Raven, they didn't kill for greed or evil; they did it to protect the ones they cared about.

"I'm sorry about your family," I offered, even though it didn't seem like enough. "I know it's not the same, but I lost my parents too. They're still alive," I clarified quickly, "But they want nothing to do with me. They housed me through high school out of obligation, but they made it known that they disagreed with my sexuality. As soon as I graduated, they asked me to leave and I never looked back."

"That's a lot like Rory and me," Dax replied with a sad smile. "The town we grew up in was narrow-minded when it came to lifestyles other than their own. We were bullied and looked down on until we were finally kicked out of our homes and families."

"But we found a new family," Rory chimed in, smiling as he looked around the table. "We're all brothers here, Wren. There's no judgement or hate; just love. We want the best for each other and look out for one another. And we'll always do the same for you."

"Thank you," I whispered, my throat tight with emotion. I'd never felt this kind of acceptance in my life. Even though it was a fucked up path to get here, I couldn't help but think this is exactly where I was supposed to be.

"You couldn't ask for a better man than Stone for a mate," Phoenix interjected. "He's strong and loyal and will protect you with his life." Stone nodded his agreement enthusiastically.

"And like any shifter, he'd move heaven and earth to make you happy," Rowan added. It was adorable how they were talking Stone up to me, even though I already thought he was great.

"*And* he kicks some serious ass," Rory insisted. "He's pretty much a weapons and fighting expert. He's a good teacher, too; he even showed Dax and me a few moves to protect ourselves."

"You did?" I whipped my head around to look at Stone, who nodded. "Could you show me some too?" I asked excitedly. Being small and weak, I was unsure what I could do, but *anything* Stone could show me would help to settle my natural anxiety.

Stone beamed with enthusiasm and pride. "I'd love to. After breakfast, I'll teach you some things." He laughed when I threw my arms around his neck in thanks.

"My god, you two are made for each other," Dax insisted, shaking his head.

Stone let me loose to cup my cheeks in his hands and rest his forehead on mine. "Yes we are." I smiled as I looked into his pretty green eyes; I was beginning to believe we were.

"Well, after your fighting lesson, would you guys like to join us later this evening for dinner?" Rory asked, interrupting our moment. "Plus, the four of us are watching sappy movies and making cookies."

"I'd like that," I answered, turning my smile on him. I usually preferred action movies over sappy ones, but what really interested me was hanging out with everyone some more. And cookies.

The others at the table gave smug looks to Stone, which I didn't understand, but Rory gave me another pearly grin. "Perfect."

Chapter Six

Wren

"How do I look?" I asked as I shuffled into the living room.

After we finished breakfast (and by finished I mean we ate every scrap of food possible - apparently we're *all* big eaters), everyone pitched in to clean the kitchen and wash the dishes. The group worked beautifully together, teasing and laughing the whole time, making their family bond obvious.

Once Stone's kitchen was spic and span, Rory walked next door to his home and collected some clothing for me since mine from the previous night were in the laundry. He said I'd be more comfortable in an outfit that fit better. His jeans were still too loose around my waist and I had to cap the pant legs so they wouldn't drag on the ground, but they fit *way* better than Stone's.

Stone's brows furrowed together at my question and his mouth opened and closed like he couldn't think of an answer. I suddenly regretted asking him; it was the first time he stopped looking at me like I put the stars in the sky.

Rory rolled his eyes and walked to my side. "There's something you need to know about shifters; they're territorial bastards. He thinks you're gorgeous, but he hates that you're wearing my clothes."

Stone nodded his agreement and I sighed in relief. "I want to get your clothes from your old home and bring them here for you," he offered, but I shook my head wildly.

"No. Please don't go there. Preston will be waiting for you. I know you're tough, but he's crazy. Please don't go there. Promise me." I was straight up losing my shit, but I couldn't stand the thought of something happening to Stone.

He crossed the room in just a few large strides and took me into his arms. "I'm sorry; I didn't mean to upset you. I promise I won't go there." I squeezed him back and nodded against his chest. "But I *do* want you to have clothing that fits you properly...and doesn't belong to another man," he added in a grumble, and snickers sounded around the room.

"I've got money in my account, but I'm afraid to buy anything with my debit card."

More quiet laughter sounded and I was confused until Stone explained, "Don't worry about that, songbird. I want to provide you with everything you need." My heart swelled; he didn't belittle my fears, and he wanted to take care of me. "Do you like to shop?"

"Are you kidding? If shopping was a sport, I'd be a gold medalist."

His chest rumbled under my face when he laughed. "Then I'd like to take you out shopping so you can choose what you like."

"That sounds amazing, but is it safe? His police buddies could be anywhere and everywhere. What if they see me? What if-"

"Shh," Stone soothed, running his hand through my hair. "You shouldn't miss out on things you enjoy because of that asshole. If you live your life in fear, he still wins. Besides, I'll never let anything happen to you." The more time we spent together, the more comfortable he seemed with showing affection and soothing me, which was especially nice considering what a scaredy cat I was.

"You're right. I can't hide forever. And even though I'm scared, I feel so safe with you," I told him honestly, and the rest of the pack replied with a collective *'aww'.*

"We'll *all* go with you, if you'd like," Rowan offered. "There's strength in numbers, and you'll have five sets of eyes on you."

"It would be our first pack date out," Dax added excitedly.

Going out as a group sounded incredible; not only for the protection, but to spend time with my new friends. But I didn't want to step on Stone's toes, so I asked him, "Is that okay with you?"

"Whatever makes you happy. Besides, I'll never turn down more protection for you."

"We can change movie night to a different day if you want to go out tonight," Phoenix offered, but I shook my head.

"No, I don't want to ruin the plans you guys already had. Is it okay if we go out tomorrow evening?"

"That works for me," Rowan answered as the rest of the group nodded.

"Sounds great," Stone cut in. "For now, I'd like to get to our lesson."

Dax snorted. "I think that's our cue to leave, guys."

Stone just nodded in agreement, but none of his friends looked offended; they just snickered and moved towards the front door. I liked all of them, but if I were honest, I was looking forward to a little alone time with Stone, and assumed he felt the same way about me. We bid the group farewell and said we'd see them soon.

"Okay, let's get down to it," Stone said once he closed the door. I narrowed my eyes in confusion when he walked past me and into the hallway, and widened them when he re-entered the living room carrying an armload of knives and holsters. "Here we go." He dumped them into a pile on the coffee table.

"Why do you prefer knives?" I asked curiously.

"I don't trust weapons with too many moving parts," he shrugged. "They can malfunction. Knives are reliable, easy to use and easy to hide." He put his hand on the small of my back and gently led me over to the table. "Try these out and see which ones you like the best."

I picked up several, testing their weight and how they felt in my hand, and decided on the two that Stone originally gave me the night before. "These aren't your favorites or anything, are they?" He *did* have them on his body when he gave them to me.

"I want you to have them," he smiled. It wasn't a 'no', which made the whole thing sweeter; Stone wanted me to feel confident and protected no matter what. "Do you like your pants tight, like the ones you wore last night?"

"You mean skinny jeans?" Stone nodded. I wasn't sure why he was curious, but I answered, "Yeah, I like how they look on me."

"Me too," Stone replied huskily, making me smile. "But they won't hide an ankle holster very well." *Ohhh.* "I want you to have these instead." He picked up two leather holsters. "This one goes on your side-" he attached it to my jeans' waistband on my left hip, "And this one goes on your back." When he hooked it onto my belt loops, it lay horizontally over the small of my back. Stone slipped the knives into their sheaths and covered them with my shirt.

"They'll be easy for you to grab, but nobody will know you have them."

"Okay, this is awesome." Stone gave me a proud grin in return.

"I'll teach you how to use them in just a minute, but there are a few other things I'd like to show you first."

"Don't you want to go outside?" I asked as Stone pushed his coffee table against the wall.

"No; I don't want you to get cold out there." My heart swelled at his words. Then Stone faced me and slapped his stomach. "Punch me."

"*What*? I can't punch you!"

"Sure you can. Come on; give it to me right in the gut."

I blinked at him. "You're serious."

"Of course I am. I don't want the first time you try to hit someone to be during a fight. You might be too scared and hold back. If you feel what it's like to actually punch a person, you'll be prepared." His reasoning made sense, but it still didn't feel right.

"I don't want to hurt you," I admitted quietly, even though it seemed *highly* unlikely, considering what a tank he was.

"You won't hurt me." He took both of my hands in his. "Please, songbird; I need to do everything I can to make sure you're safe." The mix of the nickname and his earnest plea did me in.

"Okay," I finally agreed. Stone smiled and dropped my hands.

"Go for it; as hard as you can."

I took a deep breath and cocked my fist back before ramming it into his stomach.

Pain burst across my knuckles and I yelped as I shook my hand.

"Are you okay?" Stone asked quickly. He inspected my knuckles with wide eyes before placing a gentle kiss to my skin. Any pain I felt melted away as a goofy smile crossed my lips.

"Yeah, I'm okay. Damn, you're strong; your stomach feels like a brick wall." I didn't miss the way he stood up straighter at my words.

"Let me ask you a question; would it hurt worse getting stepped on by a boot or a high heel?"

I scrunched my face up in confusion, but answered, "A high heel."

"Exactly; the pressure would be focused on one point instead of spread out. So let me show you a trick." He picked up my wrist and placed my fist against his stomach again. "You punched me like this, with all of your knuckles flat. Try rotating your wrist down just a little so that you hit me with only your first two knuckles. It will focus the pressure while protecting your hand. Hit me again."

This had to be the weirdest fucking date in history, but at the same time, it was the best one I'd ever had. Stone was showing me his strength and protective side, as well as his patience and intelligence. He was a great teacher who obviously cared about my wellbeing.

I punched his stomach again, this time holding my hand the way he showed me. It didn't hurt, and Stone let out a quiet grunt at the contact.

"That was great!" he beamed. "Did you feel the difference?" I nodded quickly; I felt powerful for the first time in my life. "Now that you know *how* to punch, let's talk about *where* to punch." He lifted my hand again and pressed my knuckles to the bridge of his nose. "If you hit someone here, their eyes will water and reduce their visibility."

My jaw dropped when he whipped his shirt off and tossed it onto the floor, giving me a view of his glorious body. Stone pressed my fingers to the center of his torso. "Do you feel the soft spot here?" It wasn't *soft* by any means, but it *was* less firm than his mounds of muscles, so I nodded. "This is the solar plexus. If you hit someone here, it can take their breath away for a minute."

Stone put his hands on my shoulders and leaned down until his eyes bore into mine. "But Wren, don't think you can only punch someone. If Preston or anyone else is trying to hurt you, you protect yourself with everything you have. Don't be afraid to fight dirty; scratch. Bite. Kick his balls. Stomp his feet. Gouge his eyes. Do whatever you have to do to survive and come home to me. I need you."

I swallowed the thick lump of emotion in my throat. Maybe Stone wasn't classically romantic, but he showed his feelings for me in the ways that really mattered. "I promise," I whispered, and he placed a tender kiss on my forehead.

I let my eyes wander back onto his body, and was once again taken aback by how stunning he was. I slowly lifted my hands and touched them to his chest. I caressed his smooth, firm skin, and Stone stood upright so I could explore more easily. My fingertips grazed over his muscles and into the grooves between them. They circled his navel and crept back up to his left pec, where a tribal patterned wolf's head was inked onto his skin.

"I love your tattoo," I told him as I traced over the swirly black lines.

"Thanks, but it's actually not a tattoo," he explained. "It's the mark of my pack. When I pledged my allegiance to Phoenix, it appeared on my skin. We all have one."

"Rory and Dax too?"

Stone nodded. "When they joined the pack, they got one too. It links us all together."

"That's really beautiful."

"I'm glad you think so, because you'll get one too when you join the pack."

"When we bond?" I blinked at how easily I said *when* and not *if.* My feelings for him were growing stronger and faster than I thought possible.

Stone smiled gently and cupped my cheek. "When we bond, it will link us and our lifelines together. The pack will accept you in at a special ceremony."

"Link our lifelines," I repeated with a nod. "That's how I'll inherit your immortality?"

"Yes. And I'll be linked to yours as well. If either of us dies, so will the other."

"*What*? Stone, I can't bond with you!" His body deflated and his eyes shone with heartache. "There's a man trying to kill me. If he takes me out, it will cost you your life. That's not a risk I'm willing to take."

An understanding smile crossed his lips and he caressed my cheek with his thumb. "Wren, listen to me; this world means nothing to me without you in it. I never want to live a day without you."

His sincerity took my breath away and sent my blood racing. I needed to show him what his words - what *he* - meant to me. I propped up onto my tiptoes while I pulled his shoulders down, and pressed my lips to his. Stone moaned quietly as his eyes slid shut.

He kept his hand on my cheek and didn't make a move to deepen the kiss. He gently pecked and nibbled my lips, kissing me slowly and tenderly. It was nothing I expected but everything I needed from my big man.

When we parted, Stone rested his forehead on mine. His eyes remained closed as he inhaled my breath and stroked my cheek. It was hands down the sweetest moment of my life.

"Well then," I finally spoke up, breaking the silence between us, "If our lives are going to be linked, we better finish my lesson." Stone gave me a proud grin.

Over the next couple of hours, he showed me a few more strikes and kicks, followed by how to block if someone tried to strike *me*. He praised me every time I used my new moves on him. The praise usually involved a kiss, so I was having a great time.

Finally, we moved on to weapons use. It took me entirely too long to figure out how to remove my knives from their holsters. I struggled to get them out of their sheaths. Then I pulled too hard on the knife in my back holster and sent it flying across the room. But Stone didn't laugh or get frustrated. He just said that's why we were practicing, and patiently showed me over and over. Eventually, I got the hang of it and he showed me how to stab with them. Even though I knew he'd heal, I refused to stab him. I felt guilty enough for doing it once already.

"Okay, you've been really gentle with me as you've taught me everything, but now I want you to really come at me." I barely had the sentence out when Stone shook his head no. "Why not? If someone is attacking me, they're not going to go easy on me. I need to see what it feels like to defend myself for real." He once again said no. "You let me hit *you*."

"That was different."

I propped my hands on my hips. "Why? Because you're not tiny and frail like me?" I wasn't trying to be rude; it was a serious question. I knew I was small. But Stone looked at me with pain in his eyes.

"Because I'd never forgive myself if I accidentally hurt you," he corrected. "Wren, you're stronger and braver than you give yourself credit for." My eyes widened and he nodded. "You got away from a man who wanted to kill you. You showed excellent survival skills with your fire. And when you learned about shifters and mates, you took it like a champ. Dax passed out when he saw Phoenix shift for the first time."

"Really?" He nodded with a smile. "Wow." My cheeks heated when I told him,

"No one's ever told me that I'm brave before." And with good reason; generally, I was afraid of my own shadow. But Stone made me feel strong. "I can't really take credit for the survival skills, though. My grandpa taught me all about that stuff."

"That's really nice. Are you two close?"

"We were," I replied, and Stone's face fell. "We were inseparable. He took me camping a lot and that's where he taught me how to build a fire and pitch a tent and all kinds of stuff. He was my best friend. He passed away when I was fifteen."

Stone pecked another kiss to my forehead. "I'm so sorry."

"Thanks. It's been five years, but it's still hard. He was more of a parent to me than my mom and dad put together. I came out to him long before I told my parents. I didn't tell them I was gay until after he died because I knew it would be a mess. Anyway, when I told my grandpa, he didn't seem shocked. We were so close, he probably knew before I did. He just told me he loved me and wanted me to be happy. He did give me a piece of advice, though."

"What was it?"

"He told me to find a man who was strong enough to protect me from the world, but respectful enough to never raise a hand to me." I gave both of his hands a squeeze. "I found him."

His lips slowly spread into a wide smile until he let out a sigh as his expression fell. "You can't seriously expect me to attack you after telling me that."

I snorted a laugh. "This is different; you're not attacking me to hurt me, you're doing it to *help* me. Please, Stone."

He gave another sigh and a little nod. "Okay, but I don't want you to hold back.

Come at me with everything you've got. Pretend I'm Preston and let me have it."

"I can do that." If anyone were to attack me, it probably *would* be Preston. And even if I could only get my revenge through imagination, I'd take it.

"Here we go."

Stone threw a right hook (though it was slowed down) and I blocked it with my forearm. A moment later, he came at me with his left arm and I blocked him again. He moved faster, punching with both hands. I stopped as many as I could, but some slipped by me. Luckily, I didn't get a fist to the face; just a light tap on the cheek or head. I knew without a doubt that Stone would never hurt me.

"Fight back," he encouraged. "If you don't incapacitate me, I'll keep coming at you." *Fuck, I hadn't thought of that.* I blocked another hook and punched him in the gut. "Yes! Again!" I pushed away another strike and rammed my fist into his solar plexus. His breath caught, but he squeaked out, "Don't stop." I stomped his foot and when he bent over, I threw an elbow into his cheek. Stone gave me a little shove. "Don't forget your weapons."

I withdrew the knife on my back in one slick movement and wrapped my fingers tightly around the handle. Stone tapped the side of my head. "Don't get distracted." He attacked again, and as I deflected him away, shallow cuts appeared on his skin from my blade, though they healed immediately. "Don't just hold your knife; use it."

"Stone, I can't stab you."

"I'm not Stone. I'm Preston." He tapped my head and then my cheek. "And right now, I'm beating the hell out of you." I slapped him away when he went for my head again. "I'm gonna kill you, Wren," he taunted, tapping the other side of my face. "Then I'm gonna kill all of your friends. I'm saving the big guy for last. He'll die slowly."

"No!" I buried my blade into his stomach until only the handle poked out. When I realized what I'd done, I gasped and covered my mouth with both hands. "Oh my god, Stone, I'm so sorry." This wasn't a shallow cut or a bony area; the knife was deep inside him, where I probably did serious damage to his organs. My eyes welled up with tears. "I was imagining Preston and when you said he'd kill you, I lost it. But *I'm* the one who hurt you. Do you need a hospital? What can I do? I'm so, so sorry!"

He wiped my cheeks dry and gazed intensely into my eyes. "I'm so fucking proud of you."

His lips descended onto mine again, but this time, he didn't kiss me slowly. He devoured my mouth, pushing my lips apart with his and sinking his tongue into my mouth. He greedily lapped against every surface and I sighed at the sweet flavor clinging to his tongue. I got on my tiptoes again to clasp the back of his head and he wrapped his arms around my waist. When he did, I felt something poking into my side.

I gasped and pushed him back when I realized it was the knife handle. "Stone, we're standing here making out when you have a knife sticking out of you!"

"Oh...right." He plucked the blade from his abdomen and I watched in awe as his skin knit back together. He shrugged and tossed the knife onto the coffee table.

"Are you okay?" He nodded with a smile. "So...can we make out again?" His smile turned wicked and he bent over to pick me up by the backs of my thighs. I wrapped my legs around his waist and he kissed me hard again.

His tongue slipped between my teeth and licked against my own. He nibbled and sucked my lips and lapped against my cheeks. When he tickled the roof of my mouth, it sent a shudder down my spine and he smiled against my lips.

My heart raced when he carried me into his bedroom and kicked the door shut behind us. When his fingers crept under the hem of my shirt, I panicked and ripped my lips from his.

"I'm sorry," he offered, quickly pulling his hands off of my back. "Was that too far?"

"No, it's not that. I..." I let out a big breath. "I have to tell you something."

"You can tell me anything." He caressed my back in soothing strokes, staying on top of my t-shirt this time.

"Do you remember what I said about not wanting to miss out with other guys?" His face dropped and he gave a subtle nod. "I didn't mean it. I only said it because...I was scared." *Imagine that.*

"What were you afraid of, songbird?"

The pet name calmed me and gave me courage to explain, "You said that you've been with a lot of guys and I...haven't. Preston was my first boyfriend and we never did anything beyond kissing." I stopped talking when a low growl rumbled in Stone's chest until he cleared his throat.

"Sorry. Go on."

"Right. So anyway, my parents never let me date and when I got out on my own, I didn't want to just jump into bed with someone. I wanted it to be special. I guess I didn't want to admit to you that I was a virgin in case my inexperience turned you away."

"Wren, do you remember what Rory said about shifters being territorial bastards?" I nodded. "You don't know how much it means to me that no man has ever touched you. I don't want to own you, and it wouldn't change my feelings for you if you'd been with someone else, but it's special to share all of your firsts with you. I wish I could give you mine. But I want you to know that nothing I've done in the past meant anything."

"I don't care about that," I told him sincerely. "Whatever you did was before you met me and if I'm honest, I'm glad you know what you're doing."

"You're incredible," he whispered before pecking my lips again.

"Well, I guess since you don't think I'm pathetic, I should be honest about something else." He nodded for me to continue. "I'm nervous. Not just because I've never done it before, but because I saw you. You're huge! And I'm so small. And one part of me in particular is tiny and that's exactly where you're gonna stick it." Stone pressed his lips together to keep from laughing and my cheeks flushed. "I know it's stupid."

"No it's not," he insisted. "I was just trying to keep from smiling over how damn proud that makes me because I know you're nervous. But Wren, you don't have to worry. I'll go slow and take care of you so you don't get hurt. And nothing happens between us until you're ready."

"You won't be upset if I say I'm not ready?"

"Of course not. I want you like crazy, but I'll never push you."

"What if I'm ready for...other stuff?"

A smile stretched his lips. "I'd say that's perfect, because I want *everything* with you."

Stone carried me to his bed and propped me onto my knees so we were almost eye level with each other. "Is it okay if I take this off?" he asked, gripping the hem of my shirt. The way he took care not to make me uncomfortable left me melted into a puddle. I gave a nod and he slowly pulled the fabric up my body and over my head, giving me time to change my mind.

"Oh, Wren," he breathed when he tossed my shirt to the floor and touched his hands to my chest. "You're beautiful." He stared reverently as he caressed over my smooth skin. Stone traced his fingers over each of my ribs, which were *just* visible beneath my flesh. I shivered when he ran the pads of his thumbs across my light pink nipples, causing them to contract into tight points.

He tickled down my stomach until his hands came to a stop at the top of my borrowed jeans. "Can I take these off too?" I nodded, but when he unbuttoned them, I put my hands on top of his.

"I'm not like you, Stone," I warned as my cheeks reddened again. "I'm not big or-" he quieted my fears with a slow, deep kiss. He sank his tongue into my mouth and my worries fluttered from my mind as he pushed the denim and my underwear over the swell of my ass, and they settled around my knees. I clung to Stone for support as I kicked them off ungracefully, and held my breath as he surveyed my body, completely bare to him.

His eyes lingered on my hard dick, and I wondered what he thought. It was only around five and a half inches long, cut and slim. It was proportionate to my frame, but I was nothing compared to Stone.

"My god, you're perfect," he whispered.

"Really?"

"Yes. You're so sexy, Wren." He pushed his sweats to the ground and I got a little thrill seeing that he wasn't wearing any underwear. The bigger thrill was seeing his huge cock standing at attention. "You see what you do to me? One look at your gorgeous body drives me crazy."

I chewed on my lip as I studied his robust form, and my hands levitated towards him on their own accord. "Can I touch you?"

"Fuck yes."

I pressed my fingers to his chiseled abdomen, but an invisible force pulled my hands down. I held my breath when I brushed against the tip of his cock, and a large drop of pre-cum slicked my fingertips. I caressed down his impressive length and cupped his balls in my palm, loving how heavy and hairy they were; Stone was undeniably manly.

"That feels so good," he whispered as I massaged his sack. I wanted to make him feel even better. I wrapped my hand around his shaft, but he was so thick that my fingers didn't meet together. I slowly stroked him root to tip, and he rested his head on his shoulders and moaned. His skin was smooth and silky, but hard as steel beneath.

Touching my sexy boyfriend had me worked up, hard, and throbbing. "Will you touch me too?" I asked desperately. I didn't want my own hand on my flesh. I wanted Stone's.

"Oh, hell yes. Let me show you something." I whimpered when Stone touched the tip of his cock to mine. My flesh jerked and pre-cum bubbled out of me and onto him. "Ohh god."

Stone gripped the base of his dick and my eyes widened as he pulled his foreskin forward to almost completely envelop my cock. His flesh was soft and warm around me.

"Holy shit, your cock just ate mine," I blurted, and Stone's chest rumbled with the deep laugh I loved. No one laughed when he wrapped his palm around our connected dicks and stroked.

Both of our cocks drooled, slicking our skin. I moaned aloud when my sensitive head rolled across Stone's. He pumped his wrist faster and my moans grew louder. I'd never felt anything like it; not only did his hand glide deliciously along my length, his foreskin sucked my heated flesh.

"Moan for me, Wren," Stone begged as he jerked us harder. "Show me how good you feel."

"Feels...incredible," I panted. Those were the only words my fuzzy brain could form. My eyes tried to roll back, but I forced them to stay open. I didn't want to miss the sight of Stone's bicep bulging as he stroked us, or the way his fiery gaze pierced into me. His strong jaw clenched and sweat beaded on his brow. "So... sexy," I grunted through my teeth.

"*You're* sexy, Wren. God, you're everything." He stroked us harder and faster, and his other hand crept down my thigh. I cried out when he cupped my balls in his palm. "You like that?"

"Yes!" He bounced my fuzzy sack as he milked my cock. Our tips wept and slipped across each other. It was almost too much; almost too good. But it was fucking perfect and I couldn't hold on. "Stone, I'm gonna come."

"Fuck yes. Come inside my cock." His hand was a blur as he jerked us in a frenzy.

"Stone, I'm coming!"

The moment my balls rolled in his palm and my cock jerked, he stilled his hand. "Watch."

I cried out his name as I erupted and my mouth remained open in shock as I watched Stone's flesh balloon up with my seed. "Jesus!" The sight was so erotic, I would've blown again if I had a single drop left.

Stone wasted no time in stroking us again, faster than ever. "That's the hottest fucking thing I've ever seen," he growled. I whimpered and gripped his chest to keep my balance when colors burst behind my eyes as he pulled my overly sensitive dick. "Gonna come, Wren."

I stared at our connected flesh when he growled out my name and exploded, impregnating his skin with his seed. He breathed in ragged breaths and rested his sweaty forehead on mine. "Amazing." I nodded my agreement enthusiastically, bouncing our noses together.

Stone slowly pulled back his foreskin, releasing our combined cum which trickled down my length and onto my balls. Before I could offer to grab a cloth, he cupped his hand around me and gently massaged the fluid into my skin. A dreamy grin crossed my lips when I realized - *he's marking me*. I wanted to be marked. I wanted to be his.

"That feels really nice," I told him, caressing over his mounded chest as he finished my rub down. "Thank you."

"Thank *you*," he countered, resting his hands on my ass. "So, um...it's almost time to go to Rory and Phoenix's place. Should we get dressed, or...?"

The man was adorable. He just gave me a brain scrambling orgasm and massaged me with his cum, but was clueless and jittery over what to do next.

"Can we cuddle for a while first? I want to be close to you."

"I'd love to. I've never cuddled before."

I wasn't surprised, but I *was* grateful; I wanted to share this very special first with him. I pulled back the blankets and patted the mattress beside me when I lay down. Stone joined me and wrapped his arms around me as I nestled my head on his chest. "How does this feel?"

"It's perfect."

I hummed and nuzzled deeper into him. "Yes it is."

Chapter Seven

Wren

After re-dressing me (grumbling the whole time about putting Rory's clothes back on me), Stone held my hand as we walked to Rory and Phoenix's home and knocked on the door.

Phoenix answered with a confused look on his face. "Since when do you knock?"

Stone huffed. "I'm *trying* to show my mate that I have manners."

"Huh. Well, come on in." When I stepped inside the cabin, I saw that it had more of a 'homey' feel than Stone's. Hunter green curtains and throw rugs brought color to the space, along with throw pillows, candles, and many photographs hung along the walls.

"These photos are gorgeous," I gushed as I took in the pictures of trees and hillsides. "Were they taken in this area?"

"Yes," Phoenix beamed. "Rory took them. He's a very talented photographer."

"He sure is."

"Oh, hey, guys!" Rory called from the kitchen, where he was working on something with Dax, who waved at us. "How did the lesson go?"

"Wren did great," Stone replied, proudly throwing his arm around me. "He stabbed me right in the stomach."

"Nice!" Dax called back, while Rory gave me a thumbs up. Phoenix patted my shoulder and Rowan congratulated me from his seat on the sofa. The group had an undeniably odd vibe, but I also couldn't deny I loved it.

"Wren, would you like to come help Dax and me with the cookies?" Rory asked.

"Sure, but I should warn you that I'm not much of a baker."

"That's okay; we'll show you." Rory was a sweetheart who went out of his way to make sure I felt welcome.

Stone kissed my temple before sending me off to my new friends, and he took a seat in a comfy-looking recliner.

Phoenix crossed his arms and squinted his eyes at my man. "Why is it every time you visit, your big ass ends up in my spot?" Stone just smirked and burrowed his big ass deeper into the chair. I chuckled all the way to the kitchen.

"Thanks for coming over to hang out with us," Rory said with a smile.

"Thanks for inviting me. But I wasn't joking when I said I wasn't a baker. I work around all kinds of yummy treats at the diner, but I don't make them; I just wait tables." I let out a sigh. "I mean, I *waited* tables. I've missed my last two shifts, so I'm definitely fired. Until now, I haven't even thought of my job...or my bills...or my house."

Rory must have noticed my panic setting in, because he put his hand on my shoulder. "I know it's difficult, but try not to worry. Stone will make sure your bills are paid and that you have everything you need; we all will. Plus, now that Stone has you, he's never going to let you out of his home."

"Jeez, Roar, you're making him sound like a kidnapper," Dax scolded, but I just laughed.

"Nah, I know what you mean. And even though it probably sounds crazy, I don't want to leave."

"It doesn't sound crazy at all," Dax insisted.

"Can I ask you guys a question?" Even though Stone told me there weren't many boundaries between packmates, I warned, "It's a little personal."

"Of course," Rory smiled.

I looked back at Stone and found that he was enthralled with his own conversation with Rowan and Phoenix, but I still whispered, "How long did it take for you to know your mate was *the one?*"

"For me, it was almost immediate," Rory answered. "Phoenix saved me after I fell off a cliff and banged myself up pretty badly. He took such good care of me, it was impossible not to fall in love with him."

"It was fast for me too," Dax added, "But I fought it at first. I was dating someone else when I met Rowan and was guilty about the feelings I had for him. But it turned out that my boyfriend was an abusive piece of shit. Rowan made me see what real love was supposed to be. He made me feel treasured and beautiful and I was gone."

I couldn't believe what the pair had been through, but I was thrilled they got their happily ever after. "Stone makes me feel treasured and beautiful too," I admitted while my cheeks flushed. "And safe. He promised to protect me from Preston and anyone else who looks at me crossways and I believe him. I'm feeling all kinds of things for him, but I've never been in love before and I didn't think it was possible to fall so quickly."

"Even though we're human, it's not hard to recognize someone who's perfectly matched to us," Rory explained. "It's easy to fall in love with someone who gives us exactly what we need. Just think; for shifters, the love is instant."

"*Instant?*" I asked with wide eyes. "You mean Stone *loves* me?" They both grinned and nodded. "Are you sure?"

"Positive. He told us."

I gasped and covered my mouth as they smiled wider. I worried why Stone hadn't told *me* until I remembered his promise to not push me into something I wasn't ready for. Maybe he was worried he'd scare me.

"Wow," I whispered through my fingers. Knowing Stone had such strong feelings for me made my heart skip a beat. "Can I ask you one more thing?" They both nodded. "Are all shifters big?" In an even quieter voice I added, "Down *there*?"

"Oh yeah," Rory and Dax both answered dreamily.

"Does it hurt?"

"Stone will take care of you," Dax assured. "It may take a little getting used to, but then holy hot damn and a jar of jam it's good." The three of us dissolved into laughter over his silly words.

"What are you three laughing about in there?" Phoenix asked, watching us from the other room with a warm smile.

"We're gossiping about our sexy mates," Rory answered, motioning for his man to turn around. The alpha blew Rory a kiss before turning back to his friends.

"Okay," Dax began, pointing to the oven, "The lasagna will be ready in just a few minutes, so we're getting dessert ready to pop in the oven when it comes out. We're making chocolate chunk cookies from scratch. Wren, will you chop this up while Rory and I mix the other ingredients?" He handed over a thick bar of chocolate.

"Sure." Rory gave me a knife and a cutting board, and I began cutting up the block while they measured and mixed. It felt great to be doing something together. Until it hurt like hell; the knife slipped and cut a gash in my index finger. "Ow, shit!"

A moment after the words left my lips, Stone was at my side. "What's wrong? Where are you hurt?" I held up my bloody finger and his eyes bulged. He gripped my wrist and led me to the sink, where he held my wound beneath cold water.

"May I see?" Rowan asked from my other side. I was so wrapped up in Stone's tender care, I didn't notice him approach. Stone kept hold of my hand as Rowan inspected my finger. "It looks pretty deep. You need stitches to close it."

Damn. "I'm sorry," I told Rory and Dax. "I really wanted to hang out tonight." It sounded like a lot more fun than driving half an hour to the closest hospital to get my finger sewn up.

"You still can," Rowan assured. "I've got everything I need to patch you up at home. It'll only take a couple of minutes."

"Really? Thanks, Row." I flinched. "Is it okay if I call you that?" I'd overheard Rory and Dax using the name, but I didn't want to overstep.

"Of course," he smiled. "Grab a seat at the table and I'll be right back." Stone led me to the dining room table and hovered over me as Rowan left the cabin and re-entered, carrying something that looked like a tackle box. He sat in a chair facing me and opened the lid of his box, revealing medical supplies.

"What can *I* do?" Stone asked, crowding into Rowan's space, still clutching onto my hand.

Rowan gave him a smile. "I just need a little space."

"Oh." Stone's body deflated and my heart sank. My big sweetheart wanted to help. "Oh, I know!" He stepped behind me and gently kneaded my shoulders. "How does that feel?"

"Incredible," I sighed. It wasn't just the massage that felt great, but Stone's desire to care for me.

Rowan gave me a wink and turned his attention back to my slit finger. He pulled a curved needle and a coil of black, silky string out of his box. "This will pinch a little."

I tucked my lip between my teeth with worry, but Dax was quick to soothe, "Don't worry, Wren; he's great at this stuff."

"Thank you, cookie," Rowan replied. The lovers shared a sweet look before getting back to their business. "Here we go."

I whimpered when he slipped the needle into my flesh, and Stone massaged deeper and kissed the top of my head.

"You're doing great, songbird. I'm right here." His presence kept me strong as Rowan stitched my wound closed. As he worked, keeping his pretty ice blue eyes on me, it was easy to see that he was the healer of the group; the caregiver.

"All done," Rowan announced as he tied off the last stitch. "Let me grab one more thing." He retrieved a jar from a cabinet before taking a strip of gauze from his box. "This is organic raw honey," he explained as he spread the jar's contents on the bandage. "It's a natural anti-inflammatory and antibacterial agent. It will help you heal more quickly." He wrapped the gauze around my wound.

"Thank you," Stone replied before I could. He kissed my head again. "You're so strong. I'm proud of you." It was just a few stitches, but his words made me feel ten feet tall.

"Here's a little something to help you feel better," Dax said as he approached. He held out a perfectly round ball of cookie dough, which I took with a smile. Cookies were best *before* they were baked, salmonella be damned. "And one for the doc," he said, feeding Rowan a ball of dough.

"Can I get one of those?" Stone asked hopefully.

Dax smiled widely before answering, "Nope," and turning away, making Rowan laugh and my big man scowl. I bit off half of my treat and held the other half up to Stone's lips. He ate it from my fingers and gave me a wink and a cheek kiss.

"Dinner's ready," Rory announced when the oven dinged loudly. "Everyone take a seat at the table please."

We munched on delicious pasta as we talked about nothing and everything. I told the pack about my grandfather and the things we did together, and we all decided to go on a camping trip together when the weather warmed up. I learned that Stone was not only a master of fighting and weapons, but also all things survival; shelter building, plant identification and scavenging. Rowan was talented with plant identification as well, though mainly for medicinal purposes. Phoenix had blazed new trails all over the forest and could identify any animal by its scent and tracks.

I was surprised and pleased to hear that they were going to teach their skills to boy scouts over the summertime at a camp they'd donated. I knew from personal experience that Stone would be an excellent teacher. I couldn't wait to see him interacting with the kids.

Of course, talking about the boy scout camp led to them telling me about its origins; how it was their old pack lands and how Raven had disrespected it, which led to details of the fight with him and his pack. Dax also told me more about his ex boyfriend Justin and how Rowan "took care" of him. Hearing their secrets made me feel closer to them, and accepted by them, like I truly was part of the pack.

After every morsel of food was devoured, we worked together and got everything cleaned up quickly. Then we waddled our full bellies into the living room.

Phoenix plopped into his recliner before Stone could get to it, and pulled Rory onto his lap. Dax and Rowan snuggled on one end of the sofa, and Stone settled onto the other end. I sat close to him, but apparently not close enough, because he cupped his hands beneath my armpits and hoisted my ass onto his thighs. He wrapped his arms around my waist and I threaded our fingers together. His lap was *way* comfier than the couch.

Rory started an ooey, gooey romantic movie as a platter of chocolate chunk cookies was passed around. I had no room in my stomach, but I ate them anyway. They were delicious; I was glad I didn't ruin them by bleeding all over the chocolate.

Throughout the movie, Rory and Phoenix and Dax and Rowan kissed and cuddled and had quiet conversations, but Stone didn't take his eyes off of the screen. I could practically hear him taking mental notes and it was adorable.

About halfway through the film, the main characters were dancing in the street as soft music played, and Stone put his lips by my ear to ask, "Would you like that?"

I smiled and whispered back, "That's nice, but not very realistic. Real romance for me is someone going to the pharmacy at nighttime to get me medicine when I'm sick, scraping the ice off of my car so I don't have to, or just holding me close while petting my hair."

"I can do that," he replied seriously. I chuckled and rested my head on his shoulder. A moment later, his thick fingers carded through my locks.

By the time the credits rolled, I was so comfortable and content, I was having trouble keeping my eyes open. "I need to get songbird home," Stone said as he stood up, scooping me into his arms. His raw strength sent a thrill through my body.

"Thanks for having us," I said through a yawn. I held up my bandaged finger. "And for this."

"No problem," Rowan insisted, still snuggling Dax tightly to his side.

"We'll see you tomorrow for our shopping date," Rory beamed.

Stone and I both bid everyone goodnight and stepped out into the freezing night.

Chapter Eight

Stone

I held Wren's body close to mine as I carried him to our cabin. It wasn't a long walk, but I wanted to keep him warm just the same.

"Thank you," he said as he climbed out of my arms when we crossed the threshold. I didn't plan on putting him down, but I supposed getting ready for bed would be easier this way.

As we brushed our teeth and went through a nighttime routine, I couldn't help but notice that Wren seemed distracted or worried. I figured he was just tired and didn't think anything of it, until we stepped into the bedroom together and his expression morphed into apprehension. After our sexy docking session and cuddling earlier, I thought Wren would want to share the bed, but I meant it when I said I wouldn't push him.

"I can take the floor again if you're not ready to sleep together."

"Huh?" Wren gave me a confused look before shaking his head. "I'm sorry; I'm kind of lost in my own little world. I was thinking about something Rory and Dax told me."

"Did they upset you?" I snarled. I loved my brothers, but I'd knock their heads together if need be.

"No, no, nothing like that," he replied quickly. "They told me something that you told them about me."

My sweet mate was talking in circles. "What did I tell them?" I'd knock *myself* in the head if I said something to worry him.

"That you love me." He blinked his big blue eyes up at me and I couldn't tell if they held hope or fear. Either way, I'd never deny my feelings for him.

"I do."

"Really?" His lips curled into a grin, and I breathed easier knowing that he wasn't freaked out by it.

"Really." I combed my fingers through his hair because I knew he liked it, and cupped my hand on the back of his neck. "I love you, Wren."

"I love you too." Now it was my turn to smile, and I hoped I didn't look creepy; every muscle in my face was pulled tight by how widely I beamed. "I asked Dax and Rory if I was a complete and total psychopath to be feeling this so quickly, but they told me it was natural between mates, even though I'm human."

That was yet another reason why I was thankful for my pack; they could help

Wren understand our culture, and answer any questions he had, even if he was too embarrassed or skittish to ask me.

"They told me something else," Wren said as he knotted his fingers in front of him. I raised my eyebrows in question and he added, "They said that all shifters were...you know...*big*, but that it feels really good." Hearing Wren talk about sex was getting me big in my pants. Little did he know, I'd seen both Rowan and Phoenix, and I was the biggest of all of us. I wasn't about to tell him that, though, seeing as he was the smallest of all of us. I didn't want to freak him out.

"We're a perfect match," I reminded him. "Our bodies were made for each other."

"That's beautiful," he replied in a whisper. Wren chewed his bottom lip for a moment before looking into my eyes and asking, "Will you make love to me?"

I fought my urge to howl and toss him onto the bed, knowing my mate needed a gentle touch. Instead, I took his cheeks in my hands and kissed him softly. I'd never kissed anyone the way I kissed Wren. Usually, kissing was just a quick, heartless warmup for the main event; a rough and rowdy ride. But kissing my mate wasn't something to be rushed. It was something to be treasured.

I slipped my tongue into his mouth and hummed happily at the flavor of peppermint toothpaste that clung to his skin. I tickled it across each ridge on the roof of his mouth, and smiled against his lips when he shivered. Our tongues tangled together, and I loved the way his curled and lapped against mine like it couldn't get enough. I inhaled his breath and swallowed his saliva, needing to take in every delicious part of the experience.

I quickly pulled Rory's clothing off of Wren's body; I didn't want anything blocking the naturally sweet aroma of my mate. My eyes rolled back in my head when I buried my nose into the crook of his neck and breathed deeply, but I peeled them open to get an uninhibited view of his beautiful bare body.

Wren worried about our size difference, but to me, he couldn't be more perfect. I loved the way one of my big hands could completely cover his hard, pretty dick. I loved the way his balls settled between his slender thighs. I loved how I could make out the curves of his bones through his smooth, creamy skin. Every inch of him was absolutely fucking perfect.

I pulled off my shirt and stepped out of my boots, and Wren thrilled me by unbuttoning my jeans. He pushed the denim to the floor and stared at my hard, throbbing cock. I'd never been a fan of underwear. I kicked my pants off to the side and patted the edge of the mattress. "Climb up here, songbird. Let me take care of you and make you feel so good."

"Yes," he breathed before settling onto his hands and knees with his ass on display. And what a gorgeous ass it was.

"Oh my god," I moaned as I took in his luscious, pale cheeks. I caressed my hands over his smooth skin, loving the way my palms covered his fleshy mounds. I gently pushed them apart and my breath caught at my first glimpse of his tiny hole. It was pink and perfect and made my mouth water so much that I couldn't resist a taste.

Wren flinched when I touched my tongue to his pucker, so I pulled back quickly. "I'm sorry; too much?" I asked when I saw his wide eyes staring back at me.

"No, it's just...was that your *tongue*?" I nodded. "What...what does it taste like?"

Ass probably wasn't the answer he was looking for, so I settled on, "Delicious," which was also true.

"Really?"

I nodded again. "Can I keep going?"

"I'm sure as hell not going to stop you. That was incredible."

If he thought one little lick was great, I was about to blow his mind. I lapped at his wrinkled flesh like a popsicle in July. I trailed the tip of my tongue along his rim, and Wren cried out when I pierced it inside him. The flavor of musk and marshmallows danced on my taste buds as I fucked him with my tongue until his body trembled.

"Oh, Stone," he chanted, pushing his ass back onto my face, begging for more. I licked his walls and sucked his hole until he clenched the blankets in a white knuckled grip and cried my name with each flick of my tongue.

Wren bucked and pleaded when I pulled away. I wanted to give him more, but I knew he could take me easier if he was worked up. "I just need to grab something," I told him before stepping to my nightstand. I pulled out a bottle of lube that had only been used for self-love. I'd never brought a man into my home.

I poured the slick liquid onto my fingers and down his crack. Wren flinched again when I touched his hole. "Easy, songbird. We're gonna take it slow." I tapped a fingertip to his pucker. "Have you ever had anything in here?"

His cheeks were pink when he looked back at me to answer, "Just my fingers." The mental image of Wren fingering himself made me dizzy.

I took a deep breath to clear my mind. "My fingers are bigger than yours, so tell me if it's too much." He nodded and faced forward, still clutching the blanket.

Wren moaned as I sank my finger into the tight heat of his ass. "Oh god, that's good." I worked my digit back and forth, gliding through his passage.

"Ready for more?"

"Yes!"

I slid a second finger in and Wren hissed through his teeth. I stilled my hand and asked, "Are you okay?" He nodded, so I slowly rocked my wrist back and forth. His tight hole sucked against my fingers, allowing me to go a little deeper each push. I scissored and circled my digits, feeling his muscles thin and loosen under my touch. "There you go. Good job, Wren." He whimpered and shuddered in thanks. "I think you're ready for me." Plus, if I held out much longer, I was going to come all over the bed. I wasn't sure if Wren was ready to complete our bond, but I was positive I needed my cum in my lover.

I poured so much lube onto my cock that it dripped onto the bed. I gripped Wren around his slim hips and lined my tip up with his hole.

"Take a deep breath and push out towards me," I instructed, and pressed forward. Wren gasped when my fat head popped through his ring of muscle. I held still and massaged his cheeks as his body swelled with deep breaths. "I won't move until you're ready," I promised.

"Okay," he said after a few moments. "I'm ready."

I tipped my hips forward, entering him ever so slowly. He whimpered as his tight hole stretched to the limit to take my girth. I massaged both of my thumbs around his rim, relaxing his flesh.

"Mm, that feels good," Wren groaned. I rubbed his skin and gently rocked my hips back and forth, inching further inside him. He hissed again and I stopped. "I...I think that's all I can take in." About three-fourths of my cock was buried in his tight little ass. "I'm sorry."

"Don't be," I pleaded. I never wanted him to feel inadequate when he was so fucking perfect it took my breath away. "You feel amazing." I wanted to make him feel amazing too, so as I rolled my hips, I reached my hand around to his weeping dick. But he already had his fingers wrapped around his length, giving himself slow pulls.

I gently batted his hand away. *I* wanted to give him all of his pleasure. I wanted to make him feel better than he ever dreamed possible. I enclosed his cock in my large palm and stroked him quickly.

"Stone, that feels so good." I jerked him faster, twisting my wrist over his sensitive tip. "Please don't stop!"

I snapped my hips quickly, making sure not to go deeper than he wanted me. "You're so fucking sexy," I grunted as I fucked him faster. "So tight and hot. You're fucking perfect, Wren."

"You...too...Stone," he panted as I shredded his little hole.

"Hell yeah, Wren; say my name." I needed to hear it on his lips; to know it was only me making him feel this way.

Wren chanted my name as I jerked his cock and pounded his ass. My flesh easily glided against his and I couldn't take my eyes off of the way his tiny hole now greedily gobbled up my dick. Sweat beaded across my brow and both of our breathing turned ragged. Wren arched his back and cried my name to the ceiling.

"Stone, I'm gonna come!"

At his words, I squeezed him tighter and stroked him faster. He bucked against me and gave a strangled cry and his cock jerked in my hand. Warm fluid trickled over my fingers and onto the bed, and his hole clenched around me. It was too tight, too warm, too perfect to fight.

"Gonna fill you up," I grunted. My balls tightened and rolled and I growled out my release. Powerful bursts of my seed shot deep into my lover, marking him as mine on the inside. Every cell in my body craved to mark him on the outside.

As if he shared my need, Wren sat up onto his knees, keeping my cock buried inside him as he rested his back on my chest. He tipped his head to the right and pleaded, "Bite me."

My fangs elongated instinctively, ready to make his wish come true, but I needed to know he wasn't just being swept away by the excitement of the moment.

"Wren, are you sure? It can't be undone."

"I'm sure. I need you, Stone. Make me yours."

My heart beat wildly in my chest and my fangs tingled with anticipation. I dropped my face to his neck and kissed the patch of creamy skin that would soon wear my mark. I curled my lips back and sank my teeth into his supple neck until I came to resistance and knew I'd hit his clavicle. Wren bucked and shuddered in my hold as he shot another powerful burst of seed onto the blankets.

I pulled my fangs free of his skin and watched as a beautiful pink mating scar appeared. I kissed the mark and Wren shivered.

"We're bonded together forever," I whispered in his ear. "I'll always love you and keep you safe. I'll do anything to make you happy, and hold you above all others. You're my life."

Water droplets splashed onto my arms and my heart squeezed when I realized my sweet mate was crying. "Songbird, are you okay?" I prayed I didn't bite too deeply into his thin frame.

"They're good tears," he hiccupped. "I can't believe this is really happening. I love you so much."

"I love you too." I wiped his face dry and rested my cheek on the top of his head. I slowly caressed my fingers up and down his stomach.

Wren shivered again and asked, "Can we snuggle under the covers?"

"Of course." We both moaned when I pulled my softening dick from his body. I pulled down the blankets and we settled onto the thick pillows. Wren cuddled into my side and I made sure he was tucked in and warm.

I tickled a hand down his back and slipped a fingertip between his cheeks. "Are you sore?" I asked, rubbing across his stretched pucker. He nodded against my chest. "I'm sorry."

"Worth it," he insisted through a yawn. "And this feels amazing." I chuckled and continued to massage his hole. My cock thickened at the touch, but my focus was only on caring for Wren. He sighed and nuzzled closer to me. "I love you, Stone."

"I love you too." I kissed his forehead and added, "Forever."

Chapter Nine

Stone

I slowly peeled my eyes open after waking from the best sleep of my life with my mate by my side. "Jesus!" I wasn't expecting to find Wren's face hovering over mine.

"I'm sorry; I didn't mean to startle you."

"It's okay." I blinked away my shock and asked, "Is something wrong?"

Wren shook his head as his cheeks flushed. "I was just looking at how handsome you are."

"Well don't let me stop you," I teased, making him chuckle.

He propped his head in one hand and ran the other through the black and gray scruff on my cheeks. "I love your beard. Do you think I'd look good with one?"

"I think you'd look good no matter what," I told him honestly.

"What about when I get all wrinkly and my balls hang to my knees?"

"I'll just have to carry them around for you," I shrugged, making him snort.

"I'm serious. I won't look as good as you when I'm eighty two."

"First of all, you'll always look *way* better than me," I argued. "And you don't have to worry about wrinkles or saggy balls; remember when I said you'd inherit some of my qualities?" He nodded. "One of those is slow aging. Once you hit about thirty five, everything slows to a stop."

"Okay, that's awesome." As soon as he said the words, his eyes widened as his stomach roared. "Sorry; I'm *super* hungry."

"You've also got my increased metabolism," I explained. "Shifting and fast healing takes a lot of energy, so we have to eat a lot of calories. You'll heal faster than a regular human, so you need to eat more too."

"So let me get this straight; I can eat as much as I want without worrying about my health, and live forever without getting brittle and crusty?" I gave him a lopsided smile and a nod. "Well damn. Finding you was definitely worth the death threat." I knew he meant the words, but he couldn't hide the trace of worry in his voice. I didn't want Wren to worry; fear never kept anyone from dying. It kept them from living.

"I've got an idea for the day," I told him with a gentle pat to his ass, careful not to hurt him since he was probably still sore. "First, I'm going to get your belly full. Then I want to put up some extra security measures around the house before we go out this evening with the pack."

"Thank you," he sighed, obviously comforted by the idea. It comforted me too; more security was never a bad thing, especially when it came to my mate.

After Wren and I got dressed (with him wearing his own outfit that I laundered for him), I fed him a gut-busting amount of pancakes and sausage, grabbed my tools out of the closet and led him outside.

"Okay," I began when we came to the treeline, "Most intruders - including Preston with his police training - will be on the lookout for typical security systems with cameras or sensors. We're going to set up things that no one will notice."

"Do you have bear traps?" Wren asked seriously. When I raised my brows in question, he nodded quickly. "If we put a bear trap down and hide it under leaves, Preston won't see it. He'll step on it and-" he clapped his hands together. "Wham! His legs will mangle and he can't run away."

I blinked wide eyes at him. "You have no idea how turned on I am right now." Hearing my sweet little Wren so hungry for revenge had all of my blood pumping south. "But unfortunately, we can't lay down traps. There's a lot of wildlife around here that could get injured."

"Right." His shoulders slumped. "I wasn't thinking."

"It was a great idea, though."

Wren beamed and hugged me around the waist. "So what are we going to do instead?"

"We're going to install alarms that will alert us if anyone is on our property. We'll point them out to the rest of the pack so they can avoid them. If an animal crosses them, it will cause a false alarm, but it won't get hurt."

"Mm, brawn *and* brains," Wren winked. I kissed him deeply before pulling some twine from my toolbox.

We worked together to tie the rope between several trees, keeping the line close to the ground. We connected them to a set of windchimes on one end and jingling bells on the other. After trying them out multiple times to make sure they worked, Wren covered the lines with fallen leaves to camouflage them.

"Great job," I told him as he dusted off his hands.

"Will we be able to hear them if we're inside?"

"My shifter hearing will pick up the sound no problem. So, now that the property is taken care of, let's go work on the cabin."

Wren watched carefully as I drilled holes into the inside of the windowsills and inserted pin locks to make the windows more difficult to open from the outside, even if an intruder had a crowbar. Then we moved on to the door; he passed me tools and complimented my handiwork as I reinforced the door jamb, making it harder for someone to kick in.

"And that's it," I said as I stashed my gear back in the closet.

Wren attached himself to my side and wrapped his arms around me. "Thank you for doing all of this. It makes me feel safe; *you* make me feel safe."

"That's all I want." I kissed him again, lingering this time as I tasted his tongue. My work was done and I wanted to take the time to show Wren what he meant to me.

I groaned when the front door swung open and my pack waltzed in. *I knew I should've locked that.*

"Sorry to interrupt," Rowan offered as I pulled my lips from Wren's. *And yet, you're still here.*

"We're just excited to go out together," Rory said with a wide smile.

"I'm looking forward to it too." Wren was too sweet to be cranky towards our nosy friends. "And to getting some new outfits." I was ready for that too; as nice as it was for Rory to lend clothing to my mate, I wanted him to have his own.

"I need to get a few pairs of jeans," Dax added, holding the waistband of the ones he wore away from his stomach. "Mine are getting a little loose."

Rowan looked aghast. "Cookie, you're losing weight? Am I not feeding you enough?"

"You are," Dax replied quickly, calming his man down. "You're just giving me lots of exercise." He flicked his eyebrows and Rowan's face relaxed into a dreamy grin before the two of them fell into a manic makeout session.

"Oh, for fuck's sake," I grumbled, and Wren lightly slapped my arm.

"I think it's sweet. They're so in love."

"They're gonna get our floor sticky if they keep it up." I had nothing against displays of affection as long as they involved me and my mate. Otherwise, I didn't need to see it.

"Come on, ya big grump," Rory said with a teasing grin as he and Phoenix stepped towards the door, and Dax and Rowan chuckled after them.

"*You* don't think I'm a grump, do you?" I asked Wren quietly. I never wanted to disappoint him.

"I think you're perfect." He crooked his finger and I leaned down for a kiss to my cheek. He loved me even though I could be surly, and that made him perfect for me.

Once we were loaded into the SUV, Rory asked Wren about his favorite type of music, and put the radio on some god awful pop station. But I overlooked the terrible music and my heart swelled at the sight of Wren, Dax and Rory dancing in their seats and singing along to the songs together. Unfortunately, Rory and Dax sounded like squealing pigs being slaughtered, though their mates appeared spellbound. My Wren, on the other hand, proved once again to be my songbird. I was grateful to have an eternity to listen to his beautiful voice.

Phoenix drove nearly an hour out of the state park and into downtown to the large shopping mall. He parked in the attached garage and we all piled out. As we walked inside the shopping center, we all stayed together, though each couple held hands. It was nice not to be a fifth wheel anymore.

Wren held my hand in a death grip and stayed glued to my side as his eyes darted all around us.

"You're safe," I told him with a squeeze to his fingers. "I promise."

"That's right," Phoenix agreed. "If someone wants you, they'll have to get through all of us, and that's not going to happen." Rory gave his man an adoring grin, and Wren's grip relaxed.

"Thank you." I gave the top of his head a kiss because why the hell not? I hoped all of the other shoppers saw and were jealous.

Dax bumped his shoulder into Wren's. "Where should we start?"

"I see where *I'm* going to start," Rowan interrupted. "I'll be right back." He hurried over to a food booth and returned with a giant soft pretzel, which he handed to Dax.

"I just fell in love with you all over again," his plump mate teased before biting off a chunk, and then feeding a bite to a very pleased Rowan.

"Thanks for bringing us all one," I grumbled, but Rowan was unaffected, and stuck his tongue out at me while Rory laughed.

"Would anyone mind if we start in there?" Wren asked, pointing to a storefront in the distance.

"Lead the way, songbird."

He led the group down the hall into a shop that had thumping music pouring from every direction and bright colors surrounded us. It was terrible, but I wanted Wren to be happy. The clothes on the rack *did* look like his style. Luckily, my mate wasn't paying any attention to the posters of half-naked male models on the walls, or I would've had to rip them down.

"Can we help you pick some things out?" Rory asked Wren hopefully.

"I'd like that."

"Great. What size pants do you wear?"

"In some styles I take a twenty-six, but I'm usually a twenty-eight."

"Holy shit!" Dax exclaimed. "Twenty six? That's like one of my thighs."

"Mm, I love your thighs," Rowan sighed, leaning down to rub his cheek against his mate's. I rolled my eyes as Wren giggled sweetly.

Dax and Rory got to work digging through the racks as their mates watched them with dumb smiles on their faces. The two of them piled their choices in Wren's arms until he could barely see over the stack of clothing. I took them from his hands and he gave me a grateful smile.

As we all trudged towards the fitting room, something caught my eye; a multicolored tie-dyed hooded sweatshirt. I lifted a size small off of the rack and held it up for Wren to see. "Will you try this on? It's bright and pretty like you."

"Aww," the others cooed, putting their hands on their chests.

I scowled at them. "Oh, shut the hell up."

Wren chuckled and took the hanger. "I love it." I beamed with pride as I helped him hang his clothes up in a dressing room. "Would you like a fashion show?"

"Obviously. I want to see them all; I know you'll look sexy in everything."

Wren lifted up on his toes for a kiss. "I'll be right out."

I was right; he looked sexy in every damn thing he put on his body. The first time he came out of the room, he smiled timidly as Rory and Dax complimented his outfit (the two of them insisted on seeing the results of their 'hard work' of shopping). Rowan and Phoenix weren't jealous as the pair made over my mate; their men were just supporting their new friend and brother, which I deeply appreciated. Especially since by the time Wren was in his last outfit, he stomped down the hall like he was king of the runway as they (and I) catcalled and whistled. They helped boost his confidence while lowering his worries.

The only problem was that as his outfits went on, his pants got tighter. That in itself was obviously not the issue; that was a goddamn gift. The problem was as I watched him, my pants got tighter too. When his tight ass swished back to the fitting room after showing off his last outfit, I couldn't hold back any longer.

"I'm going to see if he needs help getting anything back on the hanger," I lied to the group as I took off after Wren. Judging by their snickering, they knew what I was actually up to, and I gave zero fucks.

I caught the door before it closed behind Wren, and slipped into the small room with him. "Stone? What are you doing in here?"

I answered him by lightly gripping the back of his head and pulling him into a deep kiss. His eyes were unfocused when I pulled back and told him, "I want you."

"We can't do it in here." *Damn. Of course my Wren is too sweet to break the rules.* I was just about to apologize or shrug it off as a joke when he added, "We don't have any lube." *Oh my god, I love my mate.*

"We don't need any."

"Like hell we don't," he whisper-shouted back. "You're freaking huge!"

I preened a moment before telling him, "I've got other plans." His eyes bulged when I knelt in front of him.

"You mean...?"

"I haven't got to taste your pretty dick yet."

"Ohh god."

"Does that mean yes?"

Wren nodded so hard that his teeth clacked together before whispering, "But what if we get caught?"

"We won't get caught if we're quiet," I assured him. The door went down to the floor, so no one could see in. Wren covered his mouth with both hands and nodded again.

I popped the button on his jeans and pulled them and his briefs down his slender thighs. His half-hard dick lay on his fuzzy balls. *Looks like a great place to start.*

I leaned forward and pressed my tongue to his tender sack, gently lapping his flesh. His stomach surged with deep breaths as I bounced the orbs on my tongue, relishing his subtle musk on my taste buds.

His cock swelled before my eyes until it was fully hard and enticing. I licked up his shaft and swirled my tongue across his tip, collecting a salty delicious drop as Wren groaned behind his hands.

Without warning, I swallowed his cock down my throat until my lips settled against his soft blond pubic hair. Wren whimpered and watched with wide eyes as I sucked him hard, bobbing my head back and forth.

I pulled back until just his crown was between my lips, then deep throated him again and again. His body trembled and beautiful whines escaped him as he painted my tongue with pre-cum. I sucked him harder and slammed my lips into his pelvis. When I wrapped my arms behind him and squeezed two handfuls of his ass, Wren uncovered his mouth and looked down at me with wild eyes.

"Stone?" he whispered worriedly. "*Stone*?"

He was close, and I didn't want him to hold back. I nodded for him to let go, and his face stretched into a silent scream. His cock twitched and erupted, filling my mouth with bursts of his tangy seed. I swallowed it greedily, humming my approval as it slid into my stomach.

Wren gripped the walls and gasped for breath as I tucked him back into his pants. A quiet, "Wow," was all he could get out as he wiped a shaky hand down his face.

My chest rumbled with hushed laughter as I rose to my feet. I kissed his neck and whispered in his ear, "You just looked so beautiful I couldn't help myself. I always want you, Wren. I can't get enough." He smiled and pressed a sweet kiss to my lips. "Come on, songbird; let's grab these clothes and check out." I couldn't wait to spoil him by buying him every item he desired.

"Wait." He gripped my wrist to stop me from collecting the clothing. "I always want you too, you know." I sucked in a deep breath when he cupped his hand over my hard cock trapped in my jeans. "Can I try?"

"Wren, you never need to ask. Whenever, wherever and however you want to touch me, the answer is always yes please and thank you." He huffed a laugh until his gaze dropped to the thick lump behind my zipper. Then all amusement left his face and determination took over.

Wren lowered to his knees in front of me and undid my jeans to pull them halfway down my thighs. My hard, fat cock hovered in front of his eyes, and he licked his lips in anticipation.

He stretched his jaws widely to take my tip between his lips. I moaned when he flicked his tongue over my slit, and Wren gave me a panicked look. "Sorry," I whispered. "It feels so good." His eyes lit up and he licked me again, swirling his tongue over my sensitive head. I bit back another moan to keep Wren from worrying about being overheard.

He bobbed his head, sliding his lips along my length, but he couldn't take all of me into his throat. So, he wrapped one hand around my base and the other around the middle of my shaft. He worked his wrists and mouth in time, covering every inch of me in warm, smooth friction.

"Yes," I said quietly, and Wren jerked his hands quicker. I slid my fingers into his silky hair and watched as he sucked me so hard that his cheeks sank in. "So beautiful."

Wren licked, sucked and jacked my cock until my head spun and my knees went weak. My toes curled in my boots and my thighs twitched. Even though my brain was fuzzy with bliss, I managed to squeak out,

"I'm close." My mate just moved faster; he wanted to taste my seed, and knowing that made me lose control. My heavy balls rolled and lifted, and my cock pulsed as a powerful burst of cum shot into my lover's mouth. Wren swallowed over and over, taking in every drop I gave him. He dropped his hands and I shuddered when he gave my softening dick one last, long lick.

He plopped back onto his ass and I dove at him, kissing him fervently. The taste of our combined seed danced on my tongue; Wren was delicious on his own, but we were incredible together.

"That was hot," Wren whispered with an excited grin when we parted. "I feel so naughty."

I laughed out loud at my sweet man, not caring anymore who heard. After tucking all of my goodies back into my jeans, I gathered all of the clothing Wren tried on and took his hand, leading him out of the room.

To my surprise, the rest of my pack weren't in the hallway waiting for us. A quick scan of the store showed they weren't in there either.

"Where are they?" Wren asked with worry in his voice. "Do you think they got mad we took so long?"

"I'm sure they're not mad, but I don't know where-" My words cut off when I heard doors opening behind us. We turned around to find the other couples coming out of their own dressing rooms appearing cum-drunk and satisfied.

"What?" Phoenix asked, tucking Rory under his arm. "It was a great idea."

I rolled my eyes and Wren giggled all the way to the register.

Chapter Ten

Preston

"Is it all there?" I asked as Ricky sat in the passenger seat of the cruiser.

"Yep." He stashed the bag in the glove compartment and buckled his seatbelt.

Every week, we or one of our *associates* collected our money from the Winzelli Cartel, who ran drugs and illegal weapons through the city. A small group of us caught them in the act several years ago, but we worked out a great system; they paid us a cut and we looked the other way.

Just as I pulled out onto the highway, my cell phone rang, and Andrew's name flashed across the screen. "Hey, we just picked up the money," I answered. "We'll meet tonight."

"Great, but that's not why I'm calling. Stan and I got called to the mall for a shoplifter. Some bitch was trying to sneak makeup out of the store in her purse."

"So?"

"So we told her we could either take her downtown for processing or she could suck us off and we'd forget about it."

"So you're calling to brag about getting head from some bitch?"

"For one. But also to tell you that we found Wren. We've got eyes on him now."

"Why the fuck didn't you say that in the first place? Grab him."

"We can't."

"What do you mean you *can't*?"

"He's not alone. He's with a group of mostly big fuckers."

His words sent a shudder down my spine. "You don't think they're Feds, do you?"

"Nah, I think they're just his friends."

"The little shit doesn't have any friends."

"I don't know; he looks pretty friendly with them. Especially the biggest one; they're practically making out in front of everyone."

My blood boiled. I'd wanted one thing from Wren and he kept it from me. He was a total prude with me and now was being a whore in public? Fuck that.

"It sounds like he's getting too comfortable," I replied. "He needs a reminder to keep his mouth shut."

"Maybe he won't blab. He hasn't yet; maybe he's scared enough as it is."

"Do you really want to take that chance? He saw Mick. He knows all of our names. If he grows a set and talks, we're all going down. Do you want to be behind bars with the men you put there?"

"Shit, I didn't think about that. What can I do?"

"You and Stan follow them. But be discreet. If they stop again, put a tracker on their car so that we can pay them a visit later."

"Got it."

I closed the call and looked over at Ricky. "We've got a stop to make."

Chapter Eleven

Wren

"Man, I've never been this full," I groaned as I leaned back onto the booth behind me, patting my stomach.

"Never?" Stone asked, flicking his eyebrows at me. My cheeks flushed and the rest of the group snickered.

"Of food," I corrected, and Stone joined in on the laughter.

We'd just finished a huge meal at a bar and grill downtown. Stone offered to take me to a fancy restaurant, but I declined; he'd already spent way too much money on me at the mall. He bought every piece of clothing I tried on or even looked at with interest. Any time I tried to protest, he just grabbed two more items off of the rack.

Eventually, I gave in and let him spoil me. I'd never seen someone so happy to be spending money on someone else.

Of course, he probably didn't save much money at the bar and grill either, considering how much we ate. We got not only a round of burger and fries, but one of every appetizer on the menu. And we ate every bite. One good thing was that Stone, Phoenix and Rowan all wanted to provide for their mates, and decided to split the check. They all had big hearts; especially when it came to their men.

"I can drive back to the cabins," I offered to Phoenix as he finished off his second beer. Everyone else in the group had at least one beer with dinner, and I wanted to make sure we all got home safely.

The alpha gave me a kind smile. "Thank you, but it would take much more than this to impair us. We have a very high tolerance."

"I'd never put you in danger," Stone added, putting his arm around me. His lips tipped up as he caressed his fingers over my shoulder. "I love this shirt on you."

As soon as he paid for it, I changed into the multicolored hoodie that Stone picked out. It was so special to have something that my big man chose just for me, and to see how happy it made him when I wore it. I thanked him with a slow kiss to his lips.

"Oh my god," Rory said from beside me.

Stone pulled away from me and scowled at his friend. "What? You kiss *your* mate all the damn time."

"That wasn't about you two," Rory waved him off. "It was about that." He pointed towards the bar, where several televisions hung on the wall. Most of them were tuned into sports games, but one played the evening news.

My heart dropped at the image on the screen; the reporter was announcing "breaking news"; a house that had caught on fire just outside of downtown. The flames had spread to the car parked nearby, completely destroying everything in its path. Firemen were on the scene fighting the blaze, but the reporter commented that they doubted anything could be saved.

"I hope no one was hurt," Rowan remarked sadly.

Hot tears rolled down my cheeks and my pulse raced. When I sniffed my nose, Stone whipped his head around to face me with a panicked look. "Wren, what's wrong?"

I was barely able to whisper, "That's my house." Dax gasped and Rory wrapped his arm around me from my other side. "It was Preston," I insisted, finding my voice. "It's a warning. He's coming for me. I can't be here." I tried to climb over Stone to exit the circular booth, but I couldn't pass him. "Please, I need to leave. I have to go."

I had no idea *where* I needed to go, but my body twitched with the demand to move. I couldn't sit there and watch my house burn to the ground. My breathing quickened and my head spun as I tried to sort reality from my imagination. I was convinced that every person sitting in the restaurant was staring at me and reporting back to Preston. I heard him laughing all around me.

"He's going to hyperventilate," Rowan warned. "We need to get him out of here."

Stone quickly stood from the booth and took me into his arms. I wrapped my legs around his waist and my arms around his neck, clinging to him so tightly that he didn't even need to touch me, but he still held me close to him. Through blurry eyes, I saw Phoenix and Rowan toss money onto the table. They, along with Rory and Dax, followed us closely out to the SUV. Stone folded his big body into the backseat, still holding me tightly to his chest.

"Maybe it wasn't Preston," Dax suggested. He and Rory sat in the middle row and were patting my back. "Maybe it was an accident."

I thrashed my head left and right. "I left my car at his house. He took it over there and torched all of my stuff." I buried my face in Stone's neck and lost my shit, crying and snotting all over him. Stone kept one strong arm around me and combed his other hand through my hair.

"Listen to my voice," he whispered in my ear. "I'm right here with you and I'm not going anywhere." He kissed the top of my head and rocked me until I calmed in his arms. "I'm so sorry, songbird. I'm sorry about your home."

I lifted my head to look into his watery eyes. "My *home* is with you; that was just a house. Insurance will cover everything and there wasn't anything in there that can't be replaced." I'd backed up all of my photos of my grandfather on the cloud; they were the only sentimental things I owned. "I'm just upset because I'm scared. He won't stop until he finds me."

"I promise I won't let anything happen to you."

"None of us will," Rory agreed.

I turned sideways on Stone's lap so that I could see everyone in the vehicle. "I can't bring you all into this. Stone and I are already linked together, but you four can stay safe. I don't want you to risk getting hurt; don't get involved."

Dax smirked and crossed his thick arms. "Yeah, that's not gonna happen."

"You're our brother," Rowan said from the front seat. "We're all in this together."

"But Stone said there had to be a ceremony with everyone before I was in the pack."

"That's just a formality," Phoenix assured. "And what better time than the present?" *Wait, what?* "Wren, being in a pack means that you'll always have a family to protect and encourage you. We work together to care for our land. We want the best for each other, and would lay down our lives for our brothers. Do you wish to be part of this pack?"

My eyes grew misty again as I nodded. "Of course I do. Everyone has been so kind and accepting. I'm thrilled to have you all as my friends, and would be honored to have you as my family." I was still concerned about the lengths they'd go to in order to protect me, but something told me they'd do it with or without my permission.

Stone hugged me tightly and Phoenix turned to Rowan. "Do you accept Wren into our pack?" *Oh shit, there's a vote?* My asshole puckered right up and my breath caught in my chest.

"I do," Rowan answered with a smile, and I relaxed a little. "Wren, I've known Stone all of my life, and I've never seen him as happy as when he's with you. Thank you for bringing my friend joy and loving him the way he deserves. I'm proud to have you in this pack."

"Thank you," I replied in a wobbly voice as Stone bowed his head.

Phoenix patted Rowan on the back before turning to his mate. "Rory, do you accept Wren into our pack?"

Rory reached over the back of his seat to take my hand. "Yes. I know what it's like to be rejected, but how amazing it feels to find your place. You deserve that feeling too, and I hope we can give it to you."

"You already have." I leaned forward to wrap him in a big hug and he pressed a kiss to my cheek. We both chuckled when Stone pulled me back onto his lap.

"And finally, Dax, do you welcome Wren?"

"Hell yes." I launched forward and took him in a fierce hug, and he squeezed me right back. "You made our little family complete, Wren." I gave *him* a cheek kiss and quickly settled back onto Stone before he could worry.

Phoenix cleared his throat. "Wren, the group has voted unanimously, and it is my great pleasure to accept you into the Pine Ridge Pack. As your Alpha, I will guide and protect you for all time. I ask that you now show your allegiance and consent to my leadership."

Everyone smiled at me like they were waiting for something. I slowly turned my focus to Stone and whispered, "What do I do?"

"Bare your neck."

My eyes widened. "He's not going to bite me, is he?"

The others chuckled, but Stone gave me a warm grin. "No, songbird; that privilege is all mine." He nibbled on my neck until I giggled and faced forward again.

I leaned my head to the side, exposing my throat to Phoenix. It was a bit comical watching him heave his large body over the console and reach out to me. When he tapped two fingers on my neck, everyone burst into applause. They all patted my back in congratulations, and Stone once again pulled me back to him.

"Watch." He raised his shirt, revealing his glorious muscled body, along with the tattoo that covered his left pec. "This is the best part." He pushed my shirt up as well, and I gasped when the symbol on his chest emitted a soft glow.

The golden light connected us and warmed my skin. A thick black line appeared on my chest before breaking into several different branches. They swirled and danced until they formed a tribal wolf tattoo on my flesh that looked identical to Stone's, and the light faded away.

"It's beautiful," Stone hummed as he traced his finger over the design. "I love you, Wren."

"I love you too." I kissed him firmly but quickly before spinning around in my seat to face the others. "I love *all* of you."

"We love you too," Dax gushed as he and Rory pulled me into another hug. Phoenix and Rowan patted my head and Stone cuddled me from behind. I let out a happy sigh and plopped back onto my mate's lap.

"Now that *that's* all settled," Stone began, "Let's go home and make a plan to make Preston pay."

Chapter Twelve

Stone

I wanted to hold Wren on the way home, but I also wanted him to be safe, so I sat him beside me and buckled him up, but kept my arm securely around him as we drove back to our homes in the state park.

When we reached our cabin, Wren clung to me like a baby opossum as I carried him inside and took a seat at the kitchen table with him straddling my lap. He needed to be close to me, and that was something I'd happily provide.

Phoenix, Rory, Rowan and Dax sat at the table as well, casting sad smiles to my frightened mate. I couldn't imagine what he was feeling after seeing everything he owned go up in flames, and knowing it was a warning. All I knew for certain was that we had to stop Preston before he got to Wren. The man was obviously capable of anything.

Phoenix spoke before I could. "This pack doesn't attack without cause. We don't wish to cause pain or destruction to those who leave us in peace, but we also won't stand for one of our own being harassed or intimidated. Preston not only made a verbal threat against Wren, but destroyed his personal property. It's time to end this before it escalates even worse."

Phoenix's words gave me goosebumps. He was level headed and peaceful, but didn't hesitate to help one of his packmates, no matter the cost. He was a great Alpha, and I respected the hell out of him.

"What's the plan, Alpha?" Rowan asked, looking as proud as I felt to be under Phoenix's leadership.

"Wren, I need you to tell us where Preston lives," Phoenix began. "Stone, Rowan and I will go and take care of the problem as quickly and quietly as possible."

Wren rotated in my lap to face the rest of the group. "It's not just Preston. When I overheard him in his basement, he spoke of six guys; well, five, considering what happened to Mick." He squeezed my hands, which were wrapped around his waist, before continuing, "If you only take out Preston, it'll just piss the other guys off and they'll come after all of us."

"Do you know where the other men live?" I asked hopefully.

"No." Wren's body sagged. "I don't even know what they look like, except for Ricky. I've never met the others."

Phoenix rubbed his hand over his scruffy jaws as he thought. "Our only option may be to lure the men here somehow."

Wren tensed in my arms, and I ran my hands up and down his thighs in soothing strokes.

"We might not have to lure anyone," Rowan argued. "Listen."

I strained my ears. "The windchimes," I announced when I heard their distinct ring.

Wren gasped and Dax reached out for his hand. "Maybe an animal tripped the wire," he suggested, trying to calm my mate, but Phoenix shook his head.

"I hear voices...five of them."

"Oh god, it's them," Wren whispered as tears streaked his cheeks. "They found me. I led them right to you. I'm so sorry!"

"Shh, songbird; this is what we wanted," I reminded him.

"But you're not ready. You don't have a plan or-"

"I'm always ready," I told him with a wink. "It'll all be over soon." I looked at Rowan and instructed, "Get the lights." He nodded and ran to the entryway to flip the switch and conceal everything in darkness. We shifters could see perfectly in the dark, and it would give us an advantage.

After Rowan deadbolted the door, we ushered Wren, Rory and Dax into the bedroom to hide. I didn't doubt any of their fighting abilities, but the three of us were stronger, faster, and healed more quickly. I didn't want to risk any of the humans getting hurt.

Phoenix and Rowan gave their mates a swift kiss before heading back into the living room. Wren had my neck in a stranglehold.

"It'll be okay," I told him, patting his back. "I'll be okay." I *had* to be; Wren's and my lives were linked, and I wouldn't let anything happen to him. I kissed my mate firmly and peeled him off of my body, pushing him into Dax and Rory's arms. "Keep him safe." They both nodded and hugged my weeping man as I joined Phoenix and Rowan in the living room. We crouched low, not wanting to give our positions away.

Everything was quiet. It was the type of silence that made the hairs on my arms raise up in anticipation; the type that suggested it wouldn't last long, and that trouble was brewing. It was the calm before the storm.

A loud *bang* sounded on the door, but it held firm, thanks to the hardware I installed to strengthen it. Again and again the men kicked and pounded the wood, but it didn't budge. I used hand signals to communicate a plan to Rowan and Phoenix, who nodded their agreement. We crept towards the door and immediately following a thump on the wood, I threw the door open and we rushed the men waiting outside, taking them by surprise.

A tall, lanky man threw a punch at Rowan, who deflected it easily before placing a hand on either side of the man's head. After a quick jerk, he dropped the man's limp body to the ground.

A second man pointed a gun at Phoenix, but the alpha grabbed hold of his wrist and punched the underside of his arm, breaking his elbow. The man screamed in pain, but it was cut short when Phoenix took his gun from his fingers and shot him between the eyes.

"Get the big guy!" sounded to my left, and I turned just in time to see two men charging me. I wrapped one hand around each of their throats and lifted them from the ground, squeezing with all of my strength. As blood vessels burst in their eyes and their skin turned blue, they each shot several rounds into my abdomen, but I was undeterred. The bullets worked themselves out of my flesh and clattered to the ground. The men eventually stopped struggling, and I tossed their lifeless bodies onto the dirt.

"Which one of these fuckers do you think is Preston?" I asked my friends as I looked over the four bodies on the ground. *Wait; why are there only four?* The sound of breaking glass and screaming came from inside the cabin. "Wren!"

The three of us bolted back inside, and when we reached the threshold of the bedroom, my heart dropped at what I saw; the window was shattered, and a man whom I assumed to be Preston was in the room with his arm wrapped around Wren's throat from behind. Cuts covered his arms and face, making it obvious he came in through the window, and his eyes were wild.

"Get off of him, you sick fuck!" Rory yelled as he and Dax clawed at his arms, trying to pry Wren free.

Preston rammed his fist into Dax's jaw, sending him to the ground, before kicking Rory in the stomach. The two clammored to their feet, Dax's bruise already fading, as we stormed into the room with them. But we all stopped dead in our tracks when Preston pulled his gun from his side and held it to Wren's temple.

"Take one step closer and I'll blow his brains out!" Wren whimpered and Preston jostled him roughly. "Shut up!" My mate looked at me with wide, terrified eyes and it broke my heart.

"Everything's going to be alright, songbird," I told him as calmly as I could.

Preston laughed maniacally. "Don't listen to him, *songbird*," he taunted, making my blood boil. "It's not going to be alright.

You're going to pay for everything you've done."

"He didn't do anything," Rowan argued. "It was us. Let him go and deal with us."

"Shut up!" Preston screamed again, and dug the barrel of his gun into the side of Wren's face. "You just couldn't mind your own fucking business, could you?" he asked my mate. "I had a good thing going, and you took everything from me! So now, I'm going to take everything from you. But first, let's have a little fun; I'm going to tap this sweet little ass while your boyfriend watches."

Fury tore through me, but I couldn't move. If I took one step closer, Wren was a goner, and so was I. I searched my brain for something, *anything* I could do to help my mate, but was at a loss.

Preston lowered his arm from around Wren's neck and cupped his hand over his crotch. A fire ignited in my mate's eyes. Wren scrunched up his face in determination and threw his head back, slamming it into Preston's nose. Blood immediately gushed down his lips and his eyes watered. Wren threw an elbow into his ribs and managed to step away. When he did, he withdrew his knife from the holster on his back and buried it into Preston's chest.

Preston blinked in disbelief and looked down, where a handle protruded from his chest and a large red stain quickly grew on his t-shirt. He fell to his knees and rocked a moment before falling forward. The knife sank fully through him, and the tip peeked out of his back.

I ran to Wren and took him in my arms, burying my nose in the crook of his neck to breathe in his scent. He shook from head to toe and his skin was paper white.

"I...I just killed someone," he whispered.

I took his cheeks in my hands and tipped his head back so that he looked at me. "You had to, Wren. He was going to hurt you; to kill *you*. You did what you had to do and I'm so proud of you." I kissed his silky hair. "I'm sorry that I couldn't protect you. I promised, and I failed you. I pray you can forgive me."

Wren looked up at me with tears in his beautiful blue eyes. "Yes you did. You took out all of those other guys. And I never could've gotten away from Preston without what you taught me. You protected me by teaching me how to protect myself." He hugged me tightly and whispered, "I love you."

"I love you too, songbird."

"You're a badass!" Dax exclaimed as he and Rory threw their arms around my mate, interrupting our beautiful moment.

"I'm sorry we couldn't stop him from getting to Wren," Rory told me with a guilty look.

"You did all you could to keep my mate safe," I replied. "Thank you." Rory nodded and went back to hugging Wren.

"Are you okay, cookie?" Rowan asked as he examined Dax's face.

"Yeah, it doesn't even hurt anymore."

Everyone except for me stepped away from Wren when Phoenix approached. He took my mate's hand and gave him a gentle smile. "Never doubt your strength; you fought bravely. I'm proud of you, and proud to have you in my pack."

"Thank you, Alpha," Wren whispered in awe. Phoenix smiled wider and pulled him into a hug. When they parted, my mate looked at me. "What are we going to do with...the bodies?" He looked a little squeamish as he asked.

"We'll take care of them," Rowan answered for me. "You, Dax and Rory stay here and relax."

"But before we go, we need to board up the window," I insisted. It was freezing outside and I wanted Wren to stay warm.

It only took a few minutes for Rowan, Phoenix and me to nail a piece of plywood over the busted window. I'd replace the glass tomorrow, but this patch job would work for the time being. We needed to dispose of the bodies.

I took Wren in my arms again once our tools were put away. "We'll be back as soon as we can. You stay here with Dax and Rory; maybe the three of you can watch a movie together to pass the time."

Wren nodded slowly. "A movie. I can't believe we just killed five people and we're just going to sit down and watch a movie."

Rory snorted a laugh. "Welcome to a wolf pack."

*****

Rowan, Phoenix and I worked together to load the bodies into the van that the group had driven to our land, and had hidden on a dirt service road. After a quick exam of our own vehicle, we found the tracking device that led them straight to us. We figured one of them spotted us in public, but marked our car so that they could attack us later in private. We removed the tracker and stashed it in the van.

I drove the bodies to Preston's address, which Wren gave to us. Phoenix and Rowan tailed behind me in our SUV, but parked it a few blocks away. We moved swiftly, carrying the men into Preston's home under the cover of nightfall. Luckily, he didn't have any close neighbors to see what we were up to.

Once they were all seated in his living room, we wiped down every surface we may have touched, from the van to his home, to make sure we left no evidence behind.

And then we torched it all. We used gasoline to make the flames burn hotter and faster, wanting to rid the world of the filth as quickly as possible. We stuck to the shadows on the way back to our SUV, and left the area completely undetected.

When we returned home, Wren was seated between Dax and Rory, who had their arms around him as they all watched a movie. I was glad they were there to give my mate comfort when I had to be away, but I wanted him in *my* arms. When I held them out to the sides, Wren leapt from the couch and sprinted across the room. He jumped into my hold and I hugged him harder than ever before.

Rory and Dax also greeted their men with hugs, and everything was as it should be. Wren hummed as he took a deep whiff of my neck. "I love the way you smell; it's like the leather of the holsters you gave me." A laugh rumbled in my chest and he squeezed me tighter.

"Come on, sweetheart; let's give these two some privacy," Phoenix said as he led Rory towards the door. His mate nodded and gave Wren a wave goodbye.

"Don't forget; dinner at our place tomorrow," Dax said as he and Rowan also made their way outside. They all must have made plans while we were gone.

"I can't wait," Wren replied with a smile. "Goodnight, everybody."

Once the door shut, I scooped him into my arms and carried him into our bedroom. Rowan and I mopped up the blood from the floor after we boarded the window, so there were no reminders of Preston to be found.

I lovingly stripped off Wren's clothes. My cock twitched at the sight of his beautiful body, but tonight wasn't about that. As much as I wanted him, what I wanted more was to provide him comfort. I removed my clothing as well and pulled back the blankets. We climbed into bed together and Wren snuggled close to me as I tucked the covers around us.

"Are you okay?" I asked once we were comfortable.

"I am now. I was obviously terrified when Preston came bursting through the window, and for some reason, I felt a little guilty after stabbing him."

"You felt guilty because you're a better person than he could ever have dreamed of being. Even though he was threatening you, you didn't take pleasure in killing him. You're a sweet and wonderful man."

"Thank you." He nuzzled deeper into my chest. "Even though I was a little guilty at first, I'm at peace with it now. You're right; if I hadn't killed him, he would've killed me *and* you, and I couldn't let that happen. We just started our life together."

My heart swelled at his words; the fear of losing our life together gave him the strength to fight. "I want to give you the best life, Wren."

"You already have."

I smiled and kissed his head. I was just getting started; I fully intended to spoil, romance and love him for the rest of time.

Chapter Thirteen

Wren

Four weeks later

"That was so much fun," I said as Rory, Dax and I all climbed out of Dax's car. We'd just returned from one of our weekly 'mate dates'; a tradition we started a few weeks ago. Since it was Valentine's Day, we spent the afternoon watching a rom-com at the movie theater while pigging out on popcorn and candy.

When Rory first hatched the idea of 'mate dates', it took some convincing for Phoenix, Rowan and Stone to be okay with the three of us going out on our own since they wouldn't be there to protect us. But once we explained how important the dates were; that they would allow us to grow closer while giving the shifters some time together as well, our men were putty in our hands.

Of course, it also helped that Preston and his friends were no longer around to threaten me. Stone, Rowan and Phoenix disposed of their bodies by placing them in Preston's home and torching everything to ash.

When the police department launched an investigation into their deaths, they discovered a long list of nefarious activities the men were involved in. Several people came forward with claims that the officers who *should* have protected them had instead extorted or terrorized them. Unexplained large cash deposits into their bank accounts eventually linked them to the Winzelli Cartel, and it was widely believed that the gang was responsible for their deaths, though there was no evidence to charge them. Its members were, however, charged with drug trafficking, sale of illegal weapons, and money laundering, and were all behind bars. The city was a safer place with the cartel dispersed and the dirty cops gone.

"It's your turn to choose what we do next week," Dax reminded me.

"Actually, I signed us up for a cooking class. I want to surprise Stone by learning to cook something for him."

"You're so sweet," Dax replied with a smile. "And food's involved, so it sounds like a great time." I laughed and bumped my shoulder into his.

"And you're *sure* you don't want to join us for dinner tonight?" Rory asked. He, Phoenix, Dax and Rowan had reservations for a fancy fondue restaurant to celebrate the holiday.

"No thanks. Stone said he wanted a quiet night at home; I think he's planning on making me a special dinner or something."

Rory chuckled. "You've turned him into such a romantic. I never thought I'd see the day."

"I've *always* thought he was romantic," I shrugged. Rory snickered again as he and Dax took me in a tight hug.

"That's why you two are perfect together," Dax insisted. "Have a great time tonight."

"You too." The two of them kissed my cheeks and wandered off to their own cabins.

I let out a happy sigh as I climbed the stairs onto our cabin's porch. Every time I walked this path, I was met with the overwhelming sensation of coming home; all because of the man who waited for me inside. I never mourned the house that Preston destroyed because like I told Stone, it only held material items. Unlike this place, which was filled with love and memories.

This place was my home. *Stone* was my home.

Last week, I received a check from my insurance company to cover the loss of my house and car (minus my loan balances). Stone had everything I needed, so I put most of the money in the bank; except what I used to buy my lover a Valentine's gift, which I couldn't wait to give to him.

I twisted open the doorknob and my jaw dropped. The lights were dim, soft music filled the air, and red rose petals were sprinkled across the floor in a winding path. I followed the walkway through the living room and down the hall, into the bathroom, where a beautiful bouquet rested in a vase on the sink.

My heart swelled at the sight of Stone waiting for me in a bubble bath. His huge body filled the basin to the brim, but he crooked his finger, beckoning me to join him.

Stone's eyes darkened as I stripped my clothes off, tossing them to the floor. I climbed into the warm, bubbly water and sat in the only space available; on my sexy man's lap. I wrapped my arms around his neck and he groaned when his hard dick brushed against my stomach.

I rubbed my hands over his smooth scalp. "This is incredible."

"But wait; there's more," Stone replied in his best game show announcer voice. He lifted a towel from the floor and revealed a heart-shaped box of chocolates. "I've got dinner in the oven, but I don't think eating some candy first will hurt."

"Mm, I couldn't agree more." I lifted the lid from the box and fed him an orange cream filled chocolate because I knew they were his favorite.

"And one for you." He fed me a caramel because they were *my* favorite. He never forgot any tiny detail that I told him about myself. We took turns feeding each other candy until we finished the whole damn box.

I sighed and nuzzled my cheek against his. "I can't believe you did all of this for me. You're the sweetest, most perfect man in the world." At the words, my big, powerful beast of a man actually blushed, and it was the most beautiful thing I ever saw. "I've got something for you too." I leaned over the side of the tub to dig in the pocket of my discarded jeans.

"You didn't have to get me anything, songbird."

"I know I didn't *have* to; I wanted to. You're not the only one who's allowed to spoil, you know." He smirked at me until I presented him with a small black box and his expression turned surprised. "Open it."

He popped the hinged lid to find a silver ring with a wooden inlay. "Wren..." He was speechless as he stared inside the box.

"I've got this sexy scar to show everyone that I'm yours," I explained, pointing to the mating mark on my neck, "But I'd like you to have something to show that you're mine too. I picked this ring because of the wood around the center; it reminds me of all the trees around here." And his interesting obsession with the color brown, but I kept that to myself.

"I love it." Stone lifted the ring and smiled as he inspected it. He placed the box on the floor and held the jewelry out to me. "Will you put it on me?" I took the cool metal and slipped it onto his finger. Stone cupped both of my cheeks in his hands and looked deep into my eyes. "Thank you, Wren. I'm proud to wear your ring; I want everyone to know that I belong to the most beautiful, thoughtful, wonderful man on this earth."

He pulled me towards him until our lips touched. He kissed me slowly and sank his fingers into my hair. I trapped his tongue between my lips and sucked gently, tasting the sweet flavor of chocolate on his skin. A growl rumbled in his chest, vibrating against mine.

I let loose of his tongue to tell him, "I love when you do that." It was raw and powerful, but soothing at the same time. It showed that he enjoyed my touch so much that it brought out his primal side.

"Yeah?" Stone growled again, and I plastered myself to him, desperate to feel his quaking skin on every inch of mine. The gentle vibration and feel of his firm body beneath me caused my cock to swell. I shifted my hips so that our hard dicks pressed into one another. I rocked forward, and we both moaned as our heated flesh grinded together.

"Songbird, that feels amazing." Stone gripped my ass cheeks in his large hands and pulled me towards him at a steady pace. Even though we were submerged in water, I still felt the pre-cum leaking from each of us and slicking our skin. We glided effortlessly as we frot together, and my balls tingled as his hairy sack kissed mine.

My breath caught when Stone tickled a finger down my crack and over my hole, massaging my pucker until it twitched and fluttered with anticipation. His eyes burned with desire as he stared into mine. "I want you," Stone said in a gravelly voice.

"Do you have-" I didn't even finish my question before he reached over the side of the tub again and grabbed the bottle of lube that we usually kept stashed in the bedroom. Stone lifted his hips so that his cock breached the water, and I poured a generous amount of the slick liquid over his length.

Stone's eyes widened when I tossed the bottle to the floor and hovered my asshole over his tip. We'd made love dozens of times over the past month, and I'd gotten more comfortable with his colossal size. I didn't want prepped or stretched; I just wanted him and didn't want to wait.

I lowered myself down until his thick crown popped through my entrance. I hissed and sank slowly as my flesh stretched to let him in. Stone massaged my rim, relaxing my muscles and allowing me to take every inch of him until my ass cheeks settled against his thighs.

"So fucking good," Stone grunted through clenched teeth. "So tight." My skin prickled when he lowered us back into the warm water. "Ride me, Wren."

I placed my hands on his broad chest for support and bounced slowly on his cock. He filled me to my limit, pressing against my walls and providing delicious friction to my prostate. "Oh my god," I moaned as I bounced faster.

"You like my fat cock inside you?"

"Yes!"

Stone gripped my hips and guided me up and down his length. Water splashed around us and over the side of the basin, flooding the floor, but we didn't care. I tipped my head back onto my shoulders and moaned at the ceiling as pleasure overtook me. I hurled my body up and down as fast as I could, burying him inside my tight passage.

"Touch me, Stone, *please*!"

He wrapped his hand around my aching flesh, covering every inch of my dick in his wide palm. He jerked me quickly as I rocked against him, chanting his name. My toes curled and my balls tightened and lifted.

"I'm gonna come!"

"Yes!" Stone exclaimed, pumping me faster, "I want it all over me." I cried out his name as my cock erupted, painting my lover's chest with thick white gobs. I watched through heavy lidded eyes as my cum slid down his smooth chest towards the water.

Stone held my hips still and thrust up into me at a feverish pace. His thighs slapped against my ass and sent more waves cascading onto the floor. Another growl rumbled in his chest and his fingers gripped my skin. His chest heaved with ragged breaths and his brow furrowed.

"Wren!" Stone buried himself to the hilt and pumped me full of his seed, warming my insides as much as the water around me warmed my outsides. He leaned forward and sank his teeth into my mating scar, causing another burst of cum to escape me.

We trembled as we caught our breath and slowly came down from our peaks of passion. I took a washcloth from a shelf and wiped my seed from Stone's chest before snuggling into him. His cock was still inside me; I wanted him as long as possible.

I nuzzled his neck, thinking about what an amazing turn my life had taken. I had best friends in Dax and Rory, brothers in Rowan and Phoenix, and a man whose sole purpose in life was to protect me and make me happy.

He'd given me strength and bravery, and a promise of forever. I had an eternity of health and pleasure ahead of me. I was blessed beyond measure, and would never take how lucky I was for granted.

"I love you, Stone."

My big man squeezed me tighter and kissed the top of my head. "I love you too, Wren. Always."

Thank you for reading the Pine Ridge Pack series! I hope you enjoyed the books. If you did, please consider leaving a review. Look below for other titles by Jayda Marx!

Other Reads (Free with Kindle Unlimited):

M/M Paranormal Romance:

Once Bitten: Javier Coven Book 1 (Vampire M/M)

Twice Shy: Javier Coven Book 2 (Vampire M/M)

Twice Bitten: Javier Coven Book 3 (Vampire M/M/M)

Release Me: Duff Coven Book 1 (Vampire M/M) Coming soon!

Mine to Save: Pine Ridge Pack Book 1
(M/M Wolf Shifter)

Mine to Keep: Pine Ridge Pack Book 2
(M/M Wolf Shifter)

Mine to Protect: Pine Ridge Pack Book 3
(M/M Wolf Shifter)

Shadow Walker: Bay City Coven Book 1
(Vampire M/M)

Into the Shadows: Bay City Coven Book
2 (Vampire M/M)

Magic Touch (M/M Mage)

M/M Series:

Arrested Hearts Book 1: Gage & Tyson
(M/M) *Can be read as standalone

Arrested Hearts Book 2: Chris & Lyle
(M/M)

Arrested Hearts Book 3: Mike & Jonah (M/M)

Arrested Hearts Book 4: Sam & Jordan (M/M) Coming soon!

My Everything (M/M) *Can be read as standalone

My Forever (novella sequel to "My Everything") (M/M)

Head Over Wheels (M/M) *Can be read as standalone

Head Over Wheels: Book 2 (M/M)

Care for You (Head Over Wheels: Book 3) (M/M)

My Grumpy Old Bear (Loveable Grumps: Book 1) *Can be read as standalone

My Confused Cub (Lovable Grumps: Book 2)

Beautiful Dreamer (M/M Age Play)
(Secret Desires: Book 1) *Can be read
as standalone

Lost Boy (M/M BDSM) (Secret Desires:
Book 2) Coming soon!

M/M Standalone

Ours to Love (M/M/M)

Chasing Jackson (M/M)

Nervous Nate (M/M Age Play Romance)

Valentine Shmalentine (M/M)

M/F Series:

Housewife Chronicles: Complete Series
(M/F)

Luscious: Complete Series (M/F)

Made in the USA
Coppell, TX
22 June 2021